CLINKERSTONE

CLINKERSTONE

MICHAEL KEARNS

Troubador Publishing Ltd
Unit E2 Airfield Business Park,
Harrison Road, Market Harborough,
Leicestershire LE16 7UL
Tel: 0116 279 2299
Email: books@troubador.co.uk
Web: www.troubador.co.uk

ISBN 978 1 80514 477 9

British Library Cataloguing in Publication Data.
A catalogue record for this book is available from the British Library.

Printed and bound by CPI Group (UK) Ltd, Croydon, CR0 4YY
Typeset in 11pt Minion Pro by Troubador Publishing Ltd, Leicester, UK

For David El Kabir

With thanks to Barry Devlin

MORNING

Georgia…? Marion Landray… And her house. Her wreck of a mansion… The truth of it? More often than not, I wake up not knowing where the hell I am.

Time…? Not too late… Slipping in and out of sleep, aware of the pulse in my ear against the pillow, the shifting shadows on the snarled bedcovers… my half-conscious mind luring me back to Chicago. In hospital, conjuring up a picture of Charles, his poor head, scarred from the surgeon's steel.

Hospitals! Christ… I've had my share since all this began. Yesterday, or the morning before, I woke up convinced I was still in Far Point General, down here in Georgia… Of course, these inventions of the mind rarely survive the demands of getting out of bed… what with my leg still in plaster and it taking an age to get dressed.

Yea… Charles Peccatte is seldom far from my thoughts, and it's been this way since this journey into the land of his birth began. And although Chicago was where he ended his days, I feel it has been as much his adventure as mine.

Bits of his rambling soliloquies continue to rise up. I picture him in the ward, propped up in a white metal bed.

Waking me with his words, or sounds... Notes fashioned into phrases, which in turn became some sort of musical line... Those dark watery globes, alone in their inward stare, peering into a heaving, unsettled beyond... Spoken in that chesty southern drawl that I was to grow used to... Like some, forlorn, half-crazed poet, moving across the years, scraping and picking over moments of pointed experience from a past that over the following months I would gradually piece together. And his recollections repeat a shiver down my spine... one that calls up my own perceptions of a young boy's unanswered voyage. And yet, his disturbing nocturnal expressions would often give way to a morning sally which brought a smile to my face. Brings a smile now, just thinking of it.

'Contradictions!' he would roar out, twinkly eyed to a scurrying young nurse who had questioned his perplexing ways. 'I would like to think that I'm big enough to carry my share!'

I have to wonder, what if the malignant tumour hadn't overtaken him so quickly? Had he lived, I doubt this whole affair would have happened at all. Certainly not in the way that it has turned out... A half a year on I can better grasp how he drew me in, for consciously or not, that formidable if untempered mind offered more than enough to carry me into his past. But surely, not even *he* could have foreseen what it would unearth from mine.

Stretching open my sleep-filled eyes, the bedside table slowly takes form... The ammonite fossil, a childhood pendant which has lain next to my skin for... fifteen years. How many leather laces have rotted through in that time? I remember my old science teacher, Mr. Moony, explaining how the shell had been replaced by iron pyrites, fool's gold. That it was nearly two hundred million years old. The sort of fact that sticks in the mind of a child.

Truth is, it's been doing nothing but gathering dust since I got out of hospital. The desire, the habit of putting it around my neck is no longer there. So, it seems the voluted shell has done its job, its purpose laid to rest.

The room is brightening and through the open sash window a lofty cloud slips behind dark trumpets of *Ipomoea tricolor*. I can now boast a fair number of plant names in the dead language, not that I can always rely on their retrieval from such an unruly mind. The soft leafed tendrils have crept inside, and the window will no longer meet the sill without doing them damage, which is surprising given that not much more than a month ago I was despairing over their sickly state. I can still hear Marion telling me, *Leave them be, Sean! No more water. Just let the soil dry out some!* That's when I suspected her repeated plea, *I know nothing about plant husbandry.*

Last night's storm was a cracker, with the inevitable power failure. The torch – or as the Americans say, flashlight, must have rolled off the bed… There it is, beside the wardrobe. I had tried to read under its circled light before picking up the pen, one that I bought specially to set down an account of these past six months, a notion that keeps raising its head, so much so that yesterday I hobbled down to the local drugstore and bought a notebook. That's when I saw the blue fountain pen, very like the one I was given as a six-year-old on my first day at school. As for the notebook, it is thickly lined in order to prevent my explanations from wandering all over the page. But not a word have I written, for the flickering lamp got me thinking about Grandad and the candle burn on his chest from reading in bed while passing the winter nights in his leaky dwelling back in Donegal. How the hell he didn't burn himself to cinders, I'll never know.

Stretching out of the window, I look down on Zeke, still in his slippers and dressing gown. He coughs and adjusts his wheelchair. Helping him to get dressed is one of my first jobs of the day – something I am pleased to do. He likes it on the balcony, even on chilly mornings – a well-formed habit of being up with nature as it awakens. Another is reading his newspaper, commencing with the editor's views, followed by the baseball results, before settling into the crossword. This he takes seriously and if the puzzle isn't completed by lunchtime, he is not the happiest of men. Zeke is feeling his years, still in considerable pain, exhausted from all that I have put him through.

But I must get out of bed if I'm going to begin this recollection. Truth be known, I'm not at all certain of being up to the task, yet as with the adventure itself, there comes a time when a blind leap is the only way.

Ouch! My bloody leg! It keeps twinging. Itches madly under the cast… I have no right to complain. For waking each morning, quite frankly, I'm surprised to find we are still in this world.

Passing the piano, a patch of sunlight catches Charles's music, *The Lakeside Movement* as Marion has come to call it. Stained and dog-eared. And yet, the entire sonata is right here. I can still hardly believe it.

Glass and bottle in hand, with some difficulty I hobble onto the balcony, awkwardly take a seat, take a deep breath, and pour myself a drop, the dull throbbing reminding me that the cast will remain for some time yet. Charles Peccatte returns to my mind's eye – him gazing down at the hospital floor, through the floor more like.

'Home? Home is where you start from… as someone once told me', was his uncomfortable reply to my enquiry as to where he had come from, and how he'd ended up in Chicago. Little did I know that such words, from what at times seemed a mind unhinged, would become part of a puzzling verbal map that would guide me through the following months. I say guide, but more often than not it all merged into a kind of unrelenting incantation which lured me into the troubled currents of my sometimes reckless actions… As it turned out, our time together was short, yet from the outset there was a connection between us, a union that will always be there.

Put simply, I grew to love the man… And I've come to love this bloody bourbon they brew down here… As a rule, I'm not one to take a drink before noon… But it does ease the pain.

Zeke is now slumped over in his wheelchair, fast asleep in a purring snore. I never tire of the view from up here: amid the perfumed blossoms of the ancient magnolia, the descending terraces, each one a garden in its own right. Two newly planted cordylines shimmer in the light breeze, the originals long dead. Behind, leggy bushes of rosemary border the steps that lead down to the roses, ice white and pink, glowing against the solid green of an ancient yew.

The pond, now revived, carries a few fish and a spray of yellow-blossomed lilies, their large flat pads hugging the water's surface. Its serenity belies a recent upheaval, when one day I got fed up wrestling with crumbling garden walls and decided to clear the choked-up patch of stinking water.

But to my great surprise, Marion had beat me to it, for when I came down one morning, tools in hand, there she was, pulling out blanket-weed and the like, at times up to her slim waist in the primordial soup. It was a sight. Beautiful in its way. And, as strange as it may seem, I reckon that's what did it for me. That's when I began to fall for her.

Further down, a soft mossy lawn surrounds a little Greek-like temple by the stream. Too late in the morning now, but on a chilly dawn, its lead cupola floats in a gurgling cloud of bluey mist. And I cannot forget the *Elaeagnus* that has eked out a special place, having been all but swallowed up by years of ravaging bramble. Truth is, it was lucky not to be scythed down in one of my blind sweaty furies. Now its fresh silvery shoots catch the morning light, as if to call to us... whispering the wonder of it all.

To be sure, the garden is far from finished and what I've come to realise is that nature is never so, that it is continually orchestrating something else to consider. I *can* say that my toil has made a difference, and what started out as an excuse to get my foot in the door of this run-down place has ripened into something else. For even, or perhaps especially, on a wet drizzly day, it has a capacity to calm, to heal my foolish blood. Yes, it has grown into me.

Zeke opens his eyes with a wince, reflecting the continuing pain from our recent ordeal.

'Sean... is that you?'

'Yea. How's your back this morning?'

'Kinda sore,' he admits.

'Can I get you something?'

'No, no... Maybe a cold beer... But no, not before lunch,' he reconsiders, eyeing the bottle of bourbon in front of me.

'Lunch will be salmon sandwiches with dill pickles. And vanilla ice cream from the Blue Bird Café. Mrs. Drake's own.'

'Sounds fine. You gonna get out that fiddle today?'

'Maybe. A little later,' I reply, having not played a note for some weeks.

'You are makin' a good job of the garden,' he says, scanning the vista below. 'But I have already told you that.'

'And what about the wretched lawn?'

'If you keep the earth wet, the shoots will come. What day is it today?'

'Wednesday... I believe,' watching him count back to the day the seed went in.

'It's gonna be a hot one today,' he reckons, glimpsing the sun. 'Five dollars says it'll be showing itself before sundown.'

'You are on,' I answer with mock confidence, in truth not so sure of my chances.

While I look down to spy two jackdaws picking away at the subject of our bet, Zeke gazes back at the crossword, eyelids heavy, betraying a need for more rest. And with the birds' tandem flight into a slate blue sky, my sight settles on the branches of a tall, majestic poplar at the bottom of the garden, its rattling leaves barely audible as I follow a long limb into the dark massive trunk.

The stream flows behind, glittering in the light. Strange to think that this little flow links up to the rest of the moving water on this earth – that some of it will pass out into the Atlantic, might end up rolling into the coast of Donegal, to lap on the shores below the place where I was born... Water, it has always been there, in *my dream* certainly. If not a darkly breaking wave on a menacing rock, an insistent tide race, moon-driven water that ends in a hiss on an empty grey strand… But like my pendant, it too has been laid to rest, and I have *him* to thank for that.

Staring down at the clean page, it is far from clear where to begin, wary as I am of drifting off into thoughtful asides that would merely fill a dozen notebooks with rambling, formless notions… Stick to the facts, I remind myself. At times easy to recognise, although when wrapped up in the fray, not so simple. Certainly, no fanciful leaps of imagination could outdo the reality of what has unfolded, the sometimes bizarre situations in which I found myself… or often as not, put myself. Wary also of being too close to see it for what it is. Too bound up with all that has happened. And yet if I leave it for a while, for a month, say, will it mean the same thing? Will I even care to recount how Sean Gallagher ended up in this place?

Best I make a start…

CHICAGO

In December. In fact, if my memory serves me, it was the early hours of the 21st. Certainly, it turned out to be the shortest day for me, given that I was brought unconscious into the Lakeside Hospital and I didn't come around until the following night. And when I did, it was to *his* great dark voice, looming out of the ether-infused gloom. In those first few moments I had no idea where I was, nor, for that matter, who I was, and all the while the man in the next bed continued to call out what sounded like my name, albeit in a slurred, almost unintelligible drawl.

'Jean!… Jean!…You out there?… Jean?'

What kind of Hell is this? I remember thinking, unsure if I even had a physical presence, what with no apparent feeling in my limbs and my joints rusted tight. But gradually, the vague outline of a bed took shape and with some effort I pulled back the starched sheet, eased myself onto the cold linoleum floor and hobbled over to the caller's bedside. Peering down, I listened intently to the resuming sleep-talk.

'Jean… Zeke to Peps… on Fifteen… Yaku… Yakushima…'

The last of these broken words drifting back into his uncomfortable dream.

And as I continued to stare at the bedevilled face, the head shaved and freshly scarred, another voice broke the air.

'Mr. Gallagher! You should not be out of bed!' came an irritated, high-pitched command. I swivelled to see a nurse advancing, large yet light on her feet, with a golden crucifix hanging from her thick neck.

'What's with him?' I asked with difficulty, my torn tongue swollen and sore.

'Mr. Peccatte has a tumour in his head. He must not be disturbed,' she explained in a more hushed tone.

And as the strong woman took me firmly by my arm, I enquired as to where we were, she no doubt aware of my dire confusion.

'The Lakeside Hospital, in Chicago,' she answered. And as she forcefully steered me back to bed, for some reason the sight of her gold cross led me to feel for my voluted fossil and although it was still resting against my chest, my mind clicked on, sending me into a sickly foreboding.

'Nurse? My fiddle? Where the hell is my bloody fiddle?' I demanded.

She didn't appreciate such profanity, answering tersely, 'There was no such instrument when you were wheeled in!'

But the explanation was far from satisfactory, and when I demanded to know where my clothes were, she pointed to a set of lockers at one end of the dingy ward. In desperation, I staggered across the room and opened the locker in my name, but as she said, no violin! Refusing to believe it, I began pulling at the other lockers, ripping them open, one by one, frantically tearing at everything that wasn't nailed down.

In all the commotion, Mr. Peccatte had woken and with the help of a crutch, had limped right up close, those large round globes fixing me with a most penetrating stare – like he had seen me before. And as it turned out, he had. Well, heard me, being closer to the truth – busking on some godforsaken street corner of that wind-swept city. It was then that another fit of epilepsy came on, but not before the awful memory came flooding back.

I had been in a bar, drinking with someone. My fault or not, friends had been thin on the ground since arriving from Ireland. I had come to work for my uncle Francie, who runs a construction firm with, as it turned out, some *assistance* from the local Mafia. Beginning on the bottom rung as was only right, I grafted away with a pick and shovel, then as a hodman, and when one of the bricklayers took sick, I started building walls. After that it was machines: jack hammers, cement vibrators, dump trucks and the like.

Then one day Uncle Francie brought me into the office to help with the planning operations and it was not long after this that things began to go wrong. The turning point was when I came face-to-face with those *reasonable* thugs. Francie would explain or complain how it was impossible to operate without them, that they had the monopoly on cement, and if not steel, the trucks that moved it. It wasn't that they'd hold a gun to his head if he didn't play ball, it was just that they couldn't guarantee that the cement truck would show up on the right day.

In the end I couldn't stomach being under their thumb, and it finally came to a head one day when I got the job of handing over our money, money hard earned by people I had come to respect. And as I stared at that fat extortionist bending a stick of fragrant gum into his ugly mouth, I was surprised by the violence that welled up inside me, feeling the strongest urge to add the money-laden envelope to his enjoyment. So I did, shoving the whole damned wad down his throat. And I kept pushing, until his friend pulled me off and punched me out cold.

'Sean, you had better clear off for a while,' was all that Francie said when I came into work the next morning.

And so, without any real plan of where I was heading, I picked up my last pay cheque and left. I began by living off savings and when that ran out, I turned to any odd job that was going and a bit of busking and playing fiddle in a few of the Irish pubs. But I always had one eye over my shoulder, wary that those two hoods would track me down. Not a good way to live. In fact, if they only knew how close they got, for one evening when I was out busking, one of them stopped close by to do a deal with some drug pusher. It was getting dark and by then I had let my hair grow, but I was not taking any chances and slowly turned the other way. The irony was, when they had finished their business, the gum-chewer dropped a dollar into my fiddle case that was open on the ground.

It was after one of my musical pub sessions that the unthinkable happened. No, not running into the hoods, but something worse. I had put away a couple of beers on an empty stomach and was feeling pretty dreamy. The drink had gone through me like a sieve and just when I was going to ask this tin whistle player to keep an eye on my fiddle while I went off to relieve myself, he started going starry-eyed over a woman sitting at the bar. He kept repeating that he knew her from some place, and no doubt he did, or someone like her. So, thinking better of it, I took the fiddle with me.

Standing at the urinal, an old drunk kept falling into me while singing some song about the price of a dog, while sprinkling his rendition with the odd spot of barking. I use the word *singing* loosely, for the sounds that were coming out of that crooked toothless mouth were ear-wrenching at best, although strangely enough, his bark was effective, reminding me of Joey, my childhood dog back in Donegal.

The thing is, this silly song will be forever branded in my memory, marking the whole damned mess that was to follow. For, as I was propping the old guy up to keep him from sliding into a grimy urinal, a young thief was slipping out the door with my fiddle case under his arm. In a desperate reckless scurry, I tore out after him, so fast that I got myself firmly jammed in my zip. At the time I felt no pain and in my outrage the chase went on for five, maybe six blocks. It got pretty hairy as that slippery little weasel forced me over several cars in the middle of a busy intersection. Undaunted, we then sped through a little park, where despite it being near freezing the lawn was for some inexplicable reason being doused by water sprinklers. After that, it was straight through a crowd of moviegoers where I knocked someone over – an old lady, I think, and judging by the bruises on my legs, she must have protected herself with one of those Zimmer frames.

By then we were both feeling the pace, yet continued on like two rabid dogs and after another block or so I was nipping at his heels. And that's when things came to an abrupt end, when he disappeared around a blind corner, and I slammed smack into a hooker walking her beat. She was thrown onto the bonnet of a parked car, and I ended up sprawled out in the middle of the frozen road. To any passer-by, it must have appeared as one of the more pathetic sights in the history of fornication, what with me gasping for air with my bloodied trousers ripped apart, while she vented her spleen on me... and all the men she had cause to despise. And as the thief slipped off into the night with his prize, an attack of epilepsy rampaged through my mind and body. The woman cleared off in disgust... or did she pull me off the road? Despite her wrath, I have a vague feeling she did.

Looking back on it, the fit was the conclusion to a long slide of self-destruction. Not eating enough, drinking too much, on occasion indulging in the hallucinating wonders of the east, and losing what little sense I had left on a few female acquaintances. I took the hint that I had slipped below the line when the down and outs stopped bothering to trouble me for spare change.

TRANQUILLO!

One morning, a few days after the locker embarrassment, I woke up to the vague sound of a piano. The person playing was having difficulties, but still, there was something intriguing about it – lyrical moments, the likes of which I had never heard before. Unable to take the mystery any longer, I pulled on a dressing gown and went off down the corridor towards the broken, tinkling rhythms. And when I entered the hospital common room, there was the sleep-talker, hunched over a battered upright. Quietly, I crept up and peered down over his shoulder, the reason for his difficulty being immediately obvious. His left hand was no longer up to it, this no doubt due to the tumour in his head. But as he worked over the treble part, it was clear that he *had* been good, which no doubt made his frustrations all the more acute. And then, quite suddenly, he stopped, slowly turned his head and caught my eye with a look that rose out of the depths of his lonely world.

'Strange sounds,' is what I remember offering up.

And it seemed an eternity of silence before he came out with another tune. I couldn't believe my ears.

'Where did you learn—' I began to ask before he cut me short and growled.

'Jack Square! A freezing, bone-gnawing night!'

I had busked there but a few times, and I was stunned by his rendition of a lament that, as far as I knew, was personal to me and my grandfather who taught it me.

'If just one of my pupils had half the talent,' he admitted under his breath.

In such a sorry state as I was, it felt good to be appreciated, and judging by the look in his eyes it was not empty flattery, for unlike their steely penetration at the lockers, his gaze let me in, at least momentarily, before he returned to his business. And I followed his attentions to the piano stand, not a bound manuscript but a collection of grubby, dog-eared papers. It was then that I realised they were handwritten, that it was *his* music.

'So, what is this piece?' I asked during one of the rests.

'Been meaning, trying, to finish it for a long time. For too long,' he eventually shouted out over a descending passage.

With this, I began to properly appreciate the mysterious expressions which were coming out of the sorry-looking man and as he played on as best he could, I felt sickened at the sight of his obvious frustrations.

'Do you play?' he called.

'Pray?' I misheard.

'Play! The piano!'

'A little… my mother was good,' going on to explain that she all but gave it up after my father had died. And when Peccatte's penetrating stare became too much, I held out my hand and awkwardly began to introduce myself. 'I… I'm Sean, Sean Ga—'

Yet before I had finished, his head jerked back, expelling, 'Jean!' The very name which had woken me on that first night. A name that obviously had great meaning, and by the way he rolled back his eyes, someone from his past who engendered much disquiet.

For some reason I then mentioned that he didn't sound like he was from Illinois, to which he answered, 'Down south... east of the Missis... Missisi... Missississ... pi,' he kept slurring, struggling with a tongue that wouldn't connect with his injured brain. When I couldn't bare it anymore, I tried to help him out, but my poor tongue also got in a twist, having been badly bitten during the attack of epilepsy. And as our pathetic endeavours carried on, neither of us knew whether to laugh or cry at the mess we were making of the river's name. This, together with the fact that he was slobbering over the piano keys, made it all seem pathetic to the extreme. And I remember cleaning them off as best I could with the sleeve of my dressing gown.

After what seemed an interminable silence, he turned his attention back to the keyboard, playing chords which somehow echoed whatever had been going on between us, while at the same time speaking over the sounds in a haunting, lyrical manner. As for me, I became completely spellbound by it all, and then quite suddenly he turned to me once more.

'Lost him at sea,' he hoarsely whispered with eyes that sought nothing and everything... together.

'What? Who?... My father?' I queried.

Charles Peccatte continued his examination, somehow having deduced that there was more to this tragedy than I was letting on. And after he appeared to arrive at some sort of conclusion, he turned back to the keyboard and continued to play, his mind again slipping between notions.

'Ship Island,' he soon uttered. But before I could enquire any further, he reverted to that far off tone of voice, half lilting over the music's repeating rhythm, as if dredging up bits of some ancient song.

I stepped around to the back of the piano to see his face more clearly and as I did, those eyes turned up to meet my enquiring look. He continued to play on while looking at me – into me, more like – my pulse quickening, my brow growing moist.

'I reckon, once upon a time, I must have been as tall… as handsome as you?' This uttered, the suffering man drooped his damaged head and played on as best he could, his errant left hand falling rag-like over the keys.

By then my mouth was dry as dust.

'No promises, but I'll have a stab at the bass part,' I managed to nervously announce, pulling the piano stool up beside his wheelchair.

Without another word, he leafed back to the beginning and with an incisive nod, we commenced. But after only a few lines he rounded on me.

'Tranquillo!' he roared, snatching up a short stub of a pencil and scoring a heavy black line under the indication. 'Can't you hear?! Imagine, *a* composer, a man who no longer needs… wants what he knows. Or thinks he knows! Or like a child, coming upon music for the first time!'

Strangely enough, his fiery explanations settled my nerves and on the next attempt we played right through, with all but a few wee hiccups. The truth was, this remarkable music had made my blood sing and for the first time in a long while, I had forgotten my cares.

'Such a... a silence, between the sound!' is what I recall eventually stammering out. And then came the feeling, the notion, that in some odd, curious way, part of me was wrapped up in it.

There was no doubt that he too was moved by what we'd done but the whole episode had left him exhausted. Leaning back in his wheelchair, he closed his eyes and said nothing for a while, his mind drifting again, shifting discontentedly before eventually expanding on my sentiment.

'Space? Out of confinement... last move... movement. Damn thing is not right... no, not entirely there.'

For my part, the implication behind his words did not immediately sink in, still absorbed as I was in the notes. In what we had expressed.

'Last movement? You mean there is more?' I asked.

'Lost at sea, you say?' he replied, seeming not to register my question.

'I didn't say. But, yes, my father. Shipwrecked. Off the west coast of Ireland.' The fact seeming to strike a chord in his activated mind.

'On the rocks,' he continued forcibly.

'Yes. Off some cliffs, near Bloody Foreland. I doubt you know the place,' I explained while watching what little blood in his cheeks drain away.

'Cliffs. Death out of concrete cliffs,' he offered solemnly.

And with this, he gently closed the piano lid, turned his wheelchair and rolled a few paces, whereupon he cupped his good hand into the soil of a large pot plant, letting the dusty compost run slowly through his fingers. And while eying this, he drifted back into his curious, soft-spoken rhythm before moving away, me pushing his chair while he continued.

'It will take so many…'

'Begging your pardon!' I pleaded. 'What was that you said?'

'Undo so many… he said. Lost him on the rocks, you say… Boy, do you pray? Pray for those who—'

'Who said?' I interrupted.

'Lost him. Disappeared into the fog. The smoke. Washed over by the salty waves… Full fathom five thy father lies. Of his bones are coral made. Those are pearls that were his eyes! More music? Oh yes, boy. There is more.' He finished, falling fast asleep before I could even get him back to our ward.

ONCE UPON A TIME

As my tongue got better, so did my appetite, despite the daily menu of overcooked Brussels sprouts and dried up mashed potatoes. For dessert it was usually something they called cherry cobbler. Somebody should have reported them to the Ministry of Health for that one.

I admitted to having had one other more minor fit before the one that brought me in, and after doing a few tests the doctor prescribed some pills.

'Every day for the foreseeable future,' was the way he put it.

'I don't believe it!' I remember complaining. 'Every day! Until the end!'

It frightened me, never being much good at doing anything routinely, unable to even comb my hair on a regular basis.

As for Charles, he kept up his struggle with the unfinished sonata, on occasion asking my opinion as he shifted notes here and there and pondered over an ending which never seemed to satisfy him. More than once, I was woken in the middle of the night by him singing out various phrases.

'Jean... Sean! Help me up! To that miserable box they call a piano. Come, before it slips from my poor head!'

So, in the dead of night, I helped him into his wheelchair and off we went, down the long corridor to an empty common room. And if by this time we hadn't woken half the ward, our music-making certainly must have.

On the following session we even blockaded ourselves in to keep the nurses from bringing a halt to the session. I felt a certain pride, still do, when I think that my efforts made a difference. For I was right beside him, working the left-hand part as the ideas shifted and poured from his mind. And eventually, as dawn was breaking over a frosty city, we forged that ending he was searching for. I remember him turning to me with tears on his face before a big smile gradually opened up. He then held out his arms and hugged me.

And throughout the following day he needed no sleep and seemed happy as a lark. I can picture him, gazing out of the little window between our beds on a freezing cold afternoon, watching big snowflakes drifting past. And then, seemingly out of the blue, he asked about my lost violin, suggesting – no, more like ordering me to make the effort to get another. With hindsight I think he was baiting me, knowing full well that I did not want to think about the woeful episode, yet sensing that it might do me some good to talk about it.

'Something special about that fiddle?' he asked.

So, looking into those questioning eyes, there was nothing for it but to tell him how such a beautiful instrument had come to be mine.

VINCENZO PANORMO

I t was all down to my grandad, a travelling tinker whose playing was legendary in our part of the world, possessing that rare charm to bend time on its ear and make you forget your troubles. He reckoned I had inherited a piece of that talent and was most adamant about giving me lessons, especially after Dad had died.

He had set up house in part of a ruined abbey which was just offshore and a few miles up the strand from where we lived. By the time I was old enough to get around on my own, I would either skip across at low tide or row out at high.

How he came to live in this strange abode grew out of an encounter with one Father James O'Canny. According to local wisdom, he was a particularly puritan man of the cloth (some would say fanatical), who kept to the letter as regards to church policy and became a prime mover in the decline of the house dances – gatherings which people enjoyed, needed even. The story goes that one night the priest showed up at a particularly joyous poteen-driven affair and launched into one of his damnation speeches, which promptly shut the place down. My grandad was there in full spate and the two men became embroiled in a big row. So angry was Grandad that later that night, he rowed over to the abandoned church that was in earshot of O'Canny's house and commenced to play right through the night – a maelstrom of impassioned music that let no creature rest. With eyes bloodshot and his mind in a spin from a sleepless night, the priest confronted the mad fiddler the next morning, Grandad insisting that the faeries had put him up to it. Had put a spell on his fiddle. He knew full well that O'Canny detested such fallacious talk.

My grandad was a curious mixture of absolute common sense and a romantic passion that was well inside the peculiar. For one thing, he had a deep belief in the little creatures, often talking about them or claiming he saw one, the way one might notice an eagle or a stray cat. It was perfectly normal and common place, to the point that despite my inner doubts, I will admit to inheriting some sort of sympathy for the view – not that I would readily admit to such a thing.

I'm told Grandad did not stop there, but repeated the O'Canny night sessions numerous times, the two men finally coming to blows and enjoying the punch-up so much that they ended up becoming good friends. Although my grandad wasn't a believer in the traditional sense, he grew to like the abbey and when he stopped travelling about, he would spend his days there, in time roofing over one of its small chapels and keeping a few sheep on the surrounding pasture. The story goes that O'Canny and he struck a deal whereby the priest would turn a blind eye to squatting in church property and the occasional *discrete* house dance, if Grandad would slaughter him a few sheep and keep his playing to the daylight hours, or at least a normal man's bedtime.

As for the music side, Grandad was always showing me new fingerings, or unusual runs, explaining that so and so from The Blue Stacks had long ago shown him this roll, or some other great fiddler who had passed through from Sligo or Limerick had offered up this or that variation on a well-known slip jig.

I remember one morning as I was approaching the little abbey, he came out of the door with a strange glint in his eye, stranger than usual, that is.

'I was forced to break my word with O'Canny!' he called. 'Last night I was woken by some curious strumming, and I scampered out here in my skivvies to see the creature hovering over one of the rocks. The faerie was playing a little harp and beckoned me to get my fiddle. Together we fashioned out a tune,' he exclaimed, eyeing the rock where this strange event had taken place. 'The little one was *some* player and if truth be known, I was merely following his mark. And when we had done, he pointed out towards the sea stacks; I'm sure as a tribute to your father and his crew.'

Grandad then ushered me inside, picked up his fiddle and played the faerie's lament as if he had known it for years. He guided me through, after a few tries 'reversing' with him and taking the lower octave. When he was satisfied that I had it 'well placed' we had a bite to eat, and after we'd finished and were sipping our tea, he went dead quiet, as if there was something else on his mind. And as it turned out, there certainly was. For after our tea he handed me *his* fiddle to try, recounting how the Dubliner, John Boyd, his great-great-grandfather, had been given it by the maker himself as payment for getting him out of some sort of jam. I can still remember Grandad's first explanations, spoken as if he knew this violin maker first hand.

'Now this luthier, this Vincenzo, was born in Sicily way back in 1734. But he had itchy feet. A wanderer who worked in Paris and London before finally coming to this isle,' he began to explain while holding up the beautiful fiddle. 'The wood for the back came from a billiard table, would you believe! So it must have had some age before he set to carving it. Behold its form, admirable from any vantage!' He enthused, holding it up to the light of the window. 'And see how the wood glows under the varnish. With the depth of the sea itself.'

I can't help thinking that the bit about the billiard table was nothing but a fanciful ancestral anecdote, but what shone before me was like no other violin I had ever laid eyes on.

'Can you see the movement within its sureness, Sean? As if conceived in a moment yet has always existed. Still and still moving. A lesson on how you must play,' Grandad impressed upon me as he passed it gently through the air. 'You can feel the music in it.'

And he was right, for compared to my violin it had an uncanny balance in the hand, as if it had some sort of mysterious alliance with the laws of nature, with gravity itself. And I knew even before plucking it that the sound would in some way mirror this – that this Mr. Vincenzo Panormo had a rich understanding of what makes a music box.

I will never forget the moment I first ran a bow across it. For one thing, the sound was not particularly loud close in, yet as Father O'Canny knew from experience and I was to learn, its clear rich sound carried a great distance. There was a glow around the note that the ear would never tire of, a kind of sound underneath the sound, if you will. And although it was extremely quick to respond to the lightest of bow pressure, it did not give itself up all at once, there being various layers to draw upon and a certain presence that I could explore and experiment with. In total, it was a vehicle to enrich and extend the possibilities of the music.

'You will, over the years, impress your sound into it,' Grandad went on to explain, 'but it carries all who have played upon it, the man who made it and those who taught him. In this way, Sean, it is a kind of time machine.'

It wasn't long afterwards that Grandad passed it on to me, and although I left him with my poorly made box, he finished out his playing days on one made of tin, a good piece of smithery which he forged himself.

Charles seemed to enjoy my story and over the next few days we kept each other company, although his mind was, to say the least, in a variable state. I was never quite sure how much was due to the tumour or his troubled soul, things that didn't add up rising to haunt him. His way with words could be amusing; that is, if I hadn't sensed something more disturbing lurking somewhere underneath.

I remember one breakfast time he was having trouble getting some watery scrambled eggs into his mouth.

'Nurse!' he called to one young woman who was obviously new to her job. 'You call these eggs? I'd venture to say the poor hen never saw a sunrise!' he roared with a power that carried through the whole ward. And as she tried to clean him up, he continued the harassment. 'I'm not a vegetable yet! Why don't you do something useful, like give that poor fuchsia a fighting chance!' he ordered, handing her a glass of water and pointing to a little potted plant on the windowsill.

I intercepted the glass as the nurse scurried off to a more urgent command from an overworked doctor. The little plant of red-belled flowers got us talking about gardening and it soon became obvious that his knowledge ran deep on the subject. And when he found out that I used to help my mother with hers, he quizzed me until he knew the position of every flowerbed and what each contained. Even when I didn't know what the name of the plant was (which was more often than not), he would press me for a description and come up with a likely answer. But when I turned the tables and asked if he had a garden, his eyes glazed over.

'Once upon a time,' was all he would say.

FOLLOW THE MUSIC

His end came quickly. The day after our garden talk, I invited him to play the piano, but his head was too sore and his concentration span fleetingly short. The next morning, I woke to find a curtain pulled around his bed and the medics in a flutter. Later that same day, I was discharged into a Chicago that was as cold and damp as I could ever remember. I must have tramped fifty miles of pavement, trying every junk store, every pawnshop in the vain hope of finding the Panormo. In one rat-infested dump there was a violin case exactly like mine, but when I opened it up there was nothing but a roughly made, cracked up fiddle with a broken neck. No use to anyone.

I kept returning to the hospital. Two days to watch him sleep, the next to find an empty bed, his body having been efficiently taken to the basement and slid into a cold metal cupboard.

Looking back on it, I learnt little of his past, despite the fact that he wrestled with it more often than he cared to admit. Hints of it were beginning to slip out when the tumour finally got the better of him, and although I didn't always understand his half-thoughts and riddles, they never felt vacant. It was as if a kind of symbolic tongue was slowly infusing his whole being, in the end taking over to leave him no longer able to converse in a common idiom.

Living with this extraordinary consciousness, with its curious mix of courage and fear, was like trying to decipher a new language, or at least one where familiar words came out in such a way as to take on another meaning. Over those few weeks I had grown to care deeply for him, and although he never came right out and said it, I was appreciated, loved even, at a time when such things seemed abandoned, long forgotten.

I remember, standing in the entrance of that common room, staring numbly at the little battered upright, my dire situation gradually came to press home. What should I do? Stay in this city, to be hunted down by some young mobster out for his revenge? Go back to Ireland? To what? To nothing but childhood memories and ghosts. And without a hint of an answer as to what I should do with my life, I walked back to the ward in the empty hope of a miracle and that he would still be there. But when I peered in to see the two empty beds, the only thing that occurred to me was that both patients had died. It was then, as I turned to leave, that the head nurse grabbed my elbow and ushered me into her office.

'He was an interesting man. I liked him,' I heard myself say while she rummaged around on the floor, behind her desk.

'He did come out of the coma, briefly, before passing away. He wanted you to have this,' she explained dryly, producing a large paper bag and pulling out his musical effort. As I leafed through it, spotting the areas in which we worked up together, she lifted out a set of clothes. 'And these as well,' holding up a well-used tweed jacket, some matching trousers and a pair of good brogues. I took a seat. The trousers were too big but when I slid on the shoes and stood up, they felt perfect. She then helped me on with the tweed and while we were agreeing that it was a passable fit, I pulled out a watch from one of its pockets. At first, I wasn't sure what it was, for it appeared to have no face; that is, until I swivelled it over. It turned out to be a Jaeger-LeCoultre Reverso, supposedly having been designed this way to protect the face from the ravages of war. Its other special aspect, as I was to discover much later, was that it used to belong to Jean, Charles's brother.

'And one more thing,' she continued with a soft smile, now appearing to me like some sort of angel sent from heaven. 'Have a look in the breast pocket. He wrote something in it for you, towards the back.'

I pulled out a little diary and she helped to find the appropriate page, the writing in part scrawled over a faint drawing of a tree. In disbelief I read and re-read the simple instructions before looking up to see the witness's name tag pinned to her uniform.

'When I came to his bedside, the book was lying open in front of him. He just pointed to it, barely capable of asking me, but I knew what he wanted. He must have written it sometime before, except for the last bit, about the music. I offered him my pen for that, but he wanted his, which I found in the drawer of the bedside table. It was so painful to watch. It took forever for him to write it down.'

'Follow the music?' I repeated aloud. 'Did he say anything more?'

'No,' she puzzled, as we stood in silence. 'He *did* love riddles. When he first came, before his tumour got so bad, he would sometimes shout them out, even if we were just passing through the ward.'

'And his pen?'

'After he finished, he gave it to me.'

THE APARTMENT

Dressed in my new attire, I walked the dozen or so blocks to the one-room hole which had been home before landing in the hospital. When I got there, my suitcase had already been packed by the pimp of a landlord, never being one to miss a useful bed.

'The word on the street is Sean Gallagher had been snuffed out by some big-time wop,' he proceeded to tell me with a big grin, before he went on to demand the overdue rent. If my memory serves me, I had the strong desire to punch his lights out and push him right through the grimy window, but instead, I turned the argument around and demanded payment for the use of my bed sheets. In the heat of our stares, self-preservation prevailed, and we called it quits. Before I left, he even offered me a spoon full of magic mushrooms to send me on my way. Out of a can, if you please, like it was Heinz. I couldn't get out of there fast enough.

Charles Peccatte's neighbourhood was not much better than the one I had left. The address in the diary brought me to a flat-roofed apartment house – the kind that always leak. After considerable persuading, the grumpy landlord patrolled me up some creaky stairs and by the time we got to the designated door, he had decided we had something in common: my place of birth and his dog.

'My Irish wolfhound,' he cooed, gazing down at the mangy, flee-bitten creature. I wasn't about to enlighten him, but I had seen a few examples of the breed, and this one didn't come close. 'And I suppose you play the piano?' he then asked suspiciously.

'Some. Fiddle is my first instrument.'

'The fiddle!' He winced. 'Is that the same as a violin?' Before I could explain that they were one and the same thing, he retorted, 'I don't allow musicians. The only reason I let "Mr. C" stay was that he was here before I came. And he was a gentleman and could make such magic on the ivories.'

But even then, he wanted me to know that he had to put up with a lot of complaining from the other tenants, all this said to the thump of a heavy rock beat coming down the stairwell. To my mounting impatience, he eventually found the right key and despite one hell of a case of the shakes, he managed to jiggle it into the lock.

The impression as we walked in was even darker than the dingy hallway, and flicking the light switch offered little improvement. The landlord pulled back some thick, moth-eaten curtains, the grey wintry light revealing a scruffy looking Steinway grand that filled most of the room. Tucked away in an alcove was a single bed, and nearly all the wall space, including the tiny bathroom, was lined with books.

The floor creaked as he stepped up to the piano and ran his finger along the dusty keyboard lid, perhaps suddenly aware that he would never hear his former tenant again.

'As you can see, he knew plenty,' he said, waving his arm

at the wall-to-wall books. 'And what about yourself, do you read the classics?'

'No, not much,' I admitted, suddenly ashamed of my literary ignorance.

'I've got things to do. So have a look around and we can talk later.'

With the dog at his heels, he closed the door to leave me standing alone in my dead friend's world. Skimming along the bookshelves, a few of the names and titles rang vague bells from my misspent school days, but most meant nothing at all. His travel section was large and well-thumbed, like he'd been to these places and knew them. And although I had no evidence, I couldn't help feeling that this roaming had been executed alone – through parts of India, North Africa and the length and breadth of Europe; from the French coast of Normandy to the eastern borders of Poland; the Netherlands to the southern coast of Sicily.

Yes, there were books just about everywhere, except for one space where a painting, or rather a print of a painting, hung. At first, I hardly took any notice of it, but as the days passed the image began to draw me in – not because of any brightness of colour for it was, if anything, quite dull. No, it was something else, something not immediately apparent. A curious sense of rhythm – sort of like music without sound. Not that I know much about painting, but I would guess it came from the time of the Renaissance. When I turned it over a few days later there was the word *Prado* written in Charles's hand, which as I was to learn from his travel section was a distinguished picture gallery in Madrid.

The picture contained four figures, but the first impression was of a rectangle arranged in three groups. The

Virgin with the Christ child on her lap sat in the middle, with what looked like a monk standing on the left and another man on the right. He carried a staff and could have been a shepherd but for the fact that he was too well dressed for such work. There was something timeless about it all; their relative positions, the space between them being as significant as the figures themselves. Again, like impressive music, when the note makes sense only in time... before and after.

And yet the more I studied this picture, the more this harmony, this mysterious co-ordination, seemed to contradict the looks on their faces, each being separated by personal worlds of their own making, and in the case of the Christ child, a world which was yet to be. Still, there was also something that bound them together, united them in an inexplicable drama, each needing, creating the other. It all made me feel that something else was going on, something not talked about but nevertheless there, threaded into the fabric of it all.

A rotten door led to a tiny, iron-railed balcony. It was swollen stuck and flexed so much when I gave it a hefty shove that it almost came to bits as it suddenly sprung open. Covering most of the tarred floor were various potted plants, all in need of water. A tomato plant was propped up with an old golf club, a game which I couldn't imagine Charles ever playing. The plant looked dead, but there was one small tomato hanging from its crinkled stem. I picked it off and popped it in my mouth and it turned out to be one of the tastiest pieces of fruit I had ever eaten – wholly surprising how such an intense sweetness could come from such a pathetic source.

I took a seat in the solitary chair, but a cold wind soon

came whistling around my neck and brought me to my feet. Grabbing a long-spouted watering can, I quickly gave them all a drink, recalling the last time I had done such a thing, in my mother's garden, some three or four years previous. Donegal felt like another lifetime.

Back inside, I pulled Charles's music from my suitcase and placed it on the piano stand, and when I lifted the keyboard lid, I remember sensing that his presence was there, in the keys.

'His presence in the keys? What nonsense!' I recall berating. 'Next you'll be seeing faeries!'

As the memory of our duet came trickling back, I eventually took courage and began to play through about a half a page before getting snagged in a run of semiquavers. *Can't you hear? Imagine, a composer, a man who no longer needs... wants what he knows or thinks he knows*, came his fiery frustrated words. Taking a deep breath, I continued, and despite my ill-timed rendition, I did manage to glimpse what he was driving at.

Looking around the cramped apartment, I could see what he had meant by *space... out of confinement.* Playing on, I repeated some of the harder passages, coming to realise how much practice would be needed to do it justice. In truth, it felt way out of reach.

His words returned: *lost him on the rocks, you say...* which stopped me playing, my mind's eye conjuring a wave, or to be more precise, *The Wave*, as I had come to know it – a fragment of my recurring dream. Slamming into an ominous rock, it was a relic from the dreadful night that took my father's life. Not a good day for the Gallagher clan, nor the people of Baile na Bhaid.

My memory of the shipwreck hung in fragments and what I had managed to piece together came mostly from overheard pub talk. The story goes that not long after the two half deckers headed out, *An Fir Lea*, a thick dark fog descended, leaving them unable to see across the deck, let alone to the other boat. Then the storm blew in and they blindly turned for home. Uncle Jack made it to port but when my father didn't show, Jack and another boat headed back out.

By the time they sighted my dad, the gale was huge and the nets had rung the propeller dead, his boat tossing hopelessly. In trying to get in close, my uncle got caught in Dad's nets and he too sheered his prop. In the surging, dark, heaving hell, Tom Flyn's boat barely steered clear as the two others floundered into the sea stacks, the clinker-built hulls splintering up like match wood.

There hadn't been a loss like that in living memory and the only corpse that was found was our dog, Joey. He loved to go to sea. Mother has hardly ever talked about it, only to say that she scoured the beach for weeks afterwards, finding bits of hull and rope. She did come across what some claimed to be a broken bottle of holy water, which had its place in the bow of one of the boats. *An Siuloir*, my father's boat, had only one season on it and it had not long been blessed.

I was a mere thirteen. A dark, confusing time for my mother, she, like everyone else, assuming that I too had also been lost. From that day onwards I was set apart. A piece of walking folklore, not handed down from ancient times but in the here and now, living in front of their very eyes. Stories grew and spread, from me as a saint to quite the contrary.

'How in God's name could a boy of no seasoning be the

sole survivor? How did those wild waves, the fierce wind whipping up that big spring tide, let him pass back onto the land?'

Some who had lost their loved ones wanted something to blame – 'Born out of a storm, out of the cold black death of the rest. The waters will take him... will have him yet.'

I remember my grandad telling me, 'Don't you take any heed of such chatter. There are those who can spin the most dreadful yarns when they have little to do.'

I was found the next day, unconscious on one of the offshore rocks. And when I did finally come to, the whole thing had been wiped from my young mind. Imagine the state of my mother, having assumed she had lost her whole family, then to watch over her son, not knowing if he would ever open his eyes. She told me that it was two days before they could even pry open my clenched fist where the ammonite fossil was still firmly lodged. It was another two before I came around and when I did, the news of Dad's death locked my young mind solid. I don't know how long it took before they could make any sense out of me, but as our doctor claimed on more than one occasion, 'I have never seen the likes of it. No, never have.'

I played Charles's piano a little longer, but as sometimes happens, it began to feel as if I was disturbing the silence. And with this his voice returned: *yes, there is more.*

'But where?' I whispered, leaving the keyboard to look through some shelves of music. All the famous composers were there, along with many that I hadn't heard of. My pulse quickened when I opened a folder and came across a number of sheets in Charles's own hand; a good-sized piece for solo drum and voice, which seemed complete; a much more sketchy movement for string quartet; a few pages of what looked to be part of a symphony; and something which was too vague to make out – half-thoughts and scribbled out ideas. Yet look as I did, there was nothing else from the piano sonata.

I remember thinking, were these merely fragments from some larger body of work? Or was it that he didn't write much down or destroyed most of his efforts, as I could well imagine him to be too fierce a critic for his own good. But at this point, it was all blind speculation.

'Your playing? Not as good as Mr. C but it was okay... okay,' the landlord offered, suddenly perched in the doorway. I took the occasion to ask if he had ever heard anything more that could have been from the same piece. 'Sometimes he would play something... something slower. Sad it was... No, more than just sad.'

'I've looked on the shelves, but there is nothing else for solo piano from his own hand.'

'His own hand?' he repeated, not realising that Charles had actually composed the piece. 'Ah, no, maybe it was in his head. He had plenty of music up there. It's odd that he won't be returning,' he mused while we gazed uncomfortably around the room. 'His rent's due at the end of the month. After that I'll need some money. Come on, Sap,' he concluded, staring down at the dog. 'It's your dinner time.'

For the time being I was not going to worry about the legitimacy of Charles's last-minute will, and other than getting groceries from the corner store and settling a few small debts, I barely left the place. As each day passed, I became completely absorbed in this formidable collection of music and literature, growing ever more convinced that he was no ordinary man.

In point of fact, I probably read more in that month than throughout the whole of my twenty-eight years.

And I remember, as I read, my thoughts would sometimes stray to the white-scarfed head of a nun – Sister Bartholomew, my English literature teacher back in Donegal. How well she had known her subject and how rarely my mind had been on the topic at hand, although I'm damned if I can remember what did occupy it. No, I haven't retained much, other than a few of those ancient Greek gods which she would sometimes call up out of the blue, as though in some way they counterbalanced her chosen life of Catholic devotion.

Perhaps that's why she had remained in my memory, aware as I was of an active contradiction bound up within that black robe. Her curious regard for those pre-Christian gods. Zeus: 'Father Zeus who never helps liars or those who break their oaths.' And Aphrodite: 'The protectress of dewy youth.' Poseidon and his bother Hades: 'Not a welcome visitor,' as she used to warn.

And it wasn't only the gods but those who spoke of them: Homer, Hesiod, and Sophocles. The woman had views about these ancient men and a passion for their tales, and while I was holed up in my dead friend's past, I would wonder where life had taken her, my undisciplined mind picturing her on some Greek Isle, walking the shores of Crete or Ithaka.

It wasn't only novels, music and poetry that engrossed me, but that large travel section with books echoing Charles's commentary on his voyage through Europe, offering a glimpse into what at times must have been an arduous, lonely journey. There was an attraction to watery places: Venice, the reclaimed polder lands of Holland, Amsterdam and along the coast of Normandy, a place that although I did not know then, resounded with dark memory.

But I felt it wasn't all ghosts and pain, and how long he had stayed was hard to say – several years, perhaps. After France he'd made his way south over the Pyrenees and into Spain. He had even done a little teaching in Madrid, where he also researched his ancestors, for although they had come to America from France back in the eighteenth century, the name of Peccatte implied a distant Spanish descent.

I spent many a dark February night following him through the various countries, but to recount it fully would fill half a book in itself. If he wanted to stay on in a place, he usually found a café or club that would appreciate his playing. Like in Krakow at the café Michalika. And there were moments when his voyage transported me to a better clime, as on a halcyon day in Venice, imagining myself standing next to him on the steps of the Santa Maria della Salute. *Sitting happily in the warmth of the sun, surrounded by water and marble, infused in a powdery light.* Or, on the contrary, his arrival into that remarkable city, reminding me of my darkest days in Chicago: *I dragged myself out of a freezing cold night train, into an oppressive grey dawn. Staggered through the dank foetid air to find myself on some slimy marble bridge. Staring dimwit into the sickly yellow vapours that hung over the silent motionless water. As sad a case as has ever found its way to this Serenissima.*

Italy's artistic past certainly captured him – the ancient cities with their churches and galleries that housed sculptures and frescos from the seventeenth century right back to the times of antiquity. In Rome he became enthralled with the painter Caravaggio, going out of his way to search out the man's works in various chapels and private houses, *to partake of their disquieting beauty.*

But it was his encounter with another painter that I most carry with me, a man whose name will probably never be known. As I recall, this particular chain of events began when Charles found himself in Naples, broke and worn-out from all his travelling. Eventually he got a job playing in one of the restaurants, and it appears that one night his music-making pleased someone of influence, a man of high rank in the infamous Camorra. So much so that after one particularly impressive but exhausting session, the extortionist had Charles chauffeured out to the Amalfi Coast where he put him up in the Hotel Cappuccini a former convent perched high up on the cliffs. Rejuvenated, Charles was asked to stay on and more than earned his keep by playing for the guests. On the warmer nights, his hosts would make him up a bed under a colonnade of bougainvillea, and he would wake to the dawn of a purple sun rising out of the ancient waters where Homer had trimmed his sails.

He was given a bike by an old woman who could no longer ride, and he spent time exploring the various towns along the coast, living off oranges and sfogliatella – whatever that is. He was impressed by Positano, and Revello with its gardens and cloisters of San Fransesco, *founded by the very same Francis from Assisi who had inspired so many.* Further along the peninsula, some chirpy young Amalfian boy took him down into Grotta dello Smeraldo and rowed him out to witness *an emerald sea glowing unreal in the watery darkness.*

On one lazy afternoon in June, Charles decided he'd had enough of playing and so packed his bag and left the Hotel Cappuccini. This time he passed along the Gulf of Salerno in the direction of Sicily and early on one particularly fine morning, he awoke to what at first he took to be a mirage: the majesty of no less than three Dorian temples silhouetted on the horizon. Naturally he made for this ancient Greek outpost, but before arriving, he came across an archaeological dig in a farmer's field. Intrigued by the excavation of this ancient burial site, he lent a hand with the removal of a stone coffin – the remains of an Etruscan merchant who had been laid in the earth four hundred years before Christ was born. A flask to quench his thirst and a lyre made of turtle shell had been placed beside him. The coffin's walls were decorated with scenes of his afterlife, but what was unusual was that the painter had chosen to do his work on the inside. Almost immediately this find became known as The Tomb of the Diver and I understood why when I came across a photo of its lid in one of Charles's books: the deceased caught in the act of gracefully diving from one world to the next. As with the men who had first laid eyes on him, I too was deeply struck by the image – a human form so freely wrought, so confidently poised in mid-flight.

Late one evening I came across a letter from a college in Saint Louis. A Mrs. M. Yeoman, the secretary of the music department, had sent on a cheque for some back pay. And under this, a yellowed newspaper clipping with the headline *TWENTY-FIFTH ANNIVERSARY OF D-DAY LANDINGS*, this tallying with the well-thumbed travel books of Normandy and parts of Germany, and, as it turned out, something which would come to have greater meaning as the trail unfolded.

But it was a few faded black and white photographs that caught my imagination that night. One was of a large southern-style house with a partially legible address on the back, the first few letters of the town and part of the county being smeared. Another was of a woman about my age standing in a magnificent terraced garden. On the back of this was written: *M. L. 1962*. For the purpose of having something more to go on, I convinced myself that "L" meant Landray, from one of the words on the first photo. Yet this was about all I learnt of what sort of life Charles had left behind. The landlord knew nothing, as did the only one of his students of music I managed to track down.

Throughout my stay in the little apartment, his puzzling language would often return to my thoughts, and although I had nothing specific to go on, I did at moments have this nagging feeling that it referred as much to me as it did to him, that somehow his wily mind had punched an opening into my soul and had got a glimpse of something, something which although I could not put my finger on, I found deeply disturbing. This said, I could on other occasions convince myself that I was making it all up, that his mind had cut loose and gone astray, that, to be cruel, he merely revelled in the sound of his own voice. But somehow this didn't ring true, and I remember regretting that I had not tried to understand more when we were together, had not pushed him harder in his moments of calm lucidity.

Of course, I had plenty of time to wonder how he'd ended up like this, a man of such obvious talent and depth having to eke out an existence in the shadows of his chosen profession. I could find no answer, and even now I am not entirely sure. But one thing *is* certain, the whole affair revived me. For being dropped into his world put some kind of meaning back into my life, and as each day passed the desire to understand more, to *follow the music* and find the rest of the sonata, became the only thing I wanted to do.

ON THE MOVE

To add fuel to this prospect, I came across four hundred and twenty dollars that Charles had stashed away in a rusty tea caddie. After paying the landlord for another month's rent and buying a sleeping bag and some new clothes, this left me with a little over a hundred and fifty. With the sonata's last movement, the mansion and The Tomb of the Diver photographs wrapped up and placed carefully in the bottom of my travel bag, early one Sunday morning I made my way out of the city.

The plan was to hitchhike to Saint Louis where I hoped to learn something more at Black Hill College, Charles's last place of employment. Depending on what happened there, the next leg would be a boat ride down the Mississippi to Memphis, where I would then turn east, hitching again, this time through Alabama and into the state of Georgia, the rough location of the Landray Mansion.

I will always remember the morning I left Chicago, locking the door to the apartment and walking down those creaky steps into the cold, clear, wintry air. I had travelled alone before, but something had changed, for as I was waiting for a bus to the outskirts of the city, a god-awful loneliness swept through me, a despair lurking in the background which I suppose had finally come home to roost. And along with this, there was something else: an undeniable desire to be put into the hands of fate.

By the time I got to the city limits, a north wind had sealed the sky with a grey blanket of sleety rain. I stuck out my thumb for a couple of hours on interstate fifty-five before giving up. I started to walk, and it wasn't long before a beer bottle flew past my head as an open-topped convertible rattled past, its broken silencer sparking along the freeway. Not a good start, but after a few miles I came to a diner and as I was warming my hands around a cup of coffee, a trucker offered me a lift.

That first ride took me further west than planned and when he did drop me off it seemed like the middle of nowhere. I tried for another lift but as the light faded, the traffic thinned to nothing. What I remember most was the silence of it all, the kind of silence that never happens in a city, the kind of thing that I had not experienced for a very long time. It reminded me of when as a boy I would take to walking along small roads and over the peat bogs in the dead of winter. I would stop and listen, try to hear what *nothing* sounded like, sure in my heart that it would speak to me somehow. But on that strangely foreign roadside, with the temperature dropping by the minute, I soon crouched down in a ditch, crawled into my new bag and fell fast asleep.

The next morning, I was covered with an inch of snow, yet despite the conditions, the bag had done its job. I remember pulling out a squashed sausage sandwich from the suitcase and chewing away to the sight of the wind swirling the bluey white flakes across the frozen highway. The scene was strangely beautiful, and food had never tasted so good.

Not long afterwards, some guy in a transit van screeched to a stop. His radio was on so loud that it didn't allow for much conversation, and eventually he unceremoniously dropped me off just west of a place called Macombe.

The next ride was the strangest so far and I kind of knew it from the instant I got into the car, but the chance of moving forward seemed to override any sense of apprehension. The man had actually passed by once before, circling around to pick me up. A few miles down the road, while I was looking for the first signs of the famous waterway, he pulled out his cock and began to stroke it. I pretended to have tunnel vision, thinking maybe it was some sort of a tradition in this part of the world. That is, until he asked if I would like to make it flow and for some reason I put on a big smile and explained that I'd already had sausage for breakfast. After that, his driving became so erratic that at one terrifying moment our side mirror was torn away by what the Americans call "a big semi". And following this, I suggested with some force that he let me off at the next lay-by, but he seemed to have gone deaf. So, with the look in his eyes growing ever more disturbing, I helped him to apply the brakes at the first stretch of clear straight road, and where do we screech to a stop, but within a stone's throw of the great river. With what seemed like my full weight still bearing down on his foot, he was by now looking as shook up as me, and as I shoved open the door and tumbled out of the car, he wasted no time in screeching away, swerving onto the wrong side of the highway as it disappeared into the horizon. I remember it taking a little time to fully appreciate what had just occurred, but when my heart rate did eventually calm down, I actually began to feel sorry for him. Well, almost.

As I was to learn, the word Mississippi came from an old Ojibwa Indian name meaning "Great River", and once I was out of earshot of the highway, it wasn't hard to imagine it being the frontier border to the Wild West. I sat for a while, just watching the grey water, before unfolding my map in order to try and get some idea of where I was.

I began to walk along its banks and as if the day hadn't been strange enough, I eventually picked up a road and soon came upon a village signpost marked *Saint Patrick*. Despite my origins, I had never met the legend, but as I walked into the town there he was, or at least his sculpted image, standing in a green robe right next to the general store. And if this didn't drop my jaw, the next sight certainly did. A church which could have come right out of Donegal, although I can't recall one where the windows are in the shape of shamrocks. For some reason it all gave me the creeps, and after buying a hamburger and a soda I walked all the way to some other town, the name of which now escapes me. By then it was getting late, and I was relieved to get a room from a straightforward hotelier who, to my relief, wanted nothing but the usual payment.

In the morning my plan was to take a slow boat south, but instead I got a ride from some crazy rich kid in the most powerful speed boat I'd ever laid eyes on. I'm not usually nervous about fairground rides but this was something different, for no one had told this overfed, undernourished teenager that there was something in between idle and full throttle. I could smell his inner frustration and to swallow half of his bragging would be to believe that his father owned most of Illinois and was next in line for governorship. He, with his locked-on grin, kept telling me how much he respected the rich man, although I had to doubt he had much love for him. To my great relief, he dropped me off in one piece at a town called Quincy, and with a hail of, 'Good luck, partner!' he disappeared back upstream in the blink of an eye – no doubt grinning all the way.

The next ride couldn't have been more different, for I managed to talk my way onto a cargo boat – slow and steady, and I was glad of it. Here I met Hoxie Rolla, the fifteen stone black captain who, I was to learn, had hardly ever been out of eyesight of the great river. Passing by a pretty white town on the right bank, I will never forget him catching my eye and proclaiming "Hannibal", as if it should have meant something.

'The home of Sam Clemens.' Yet still I remained ignorant. 'Mark Twain!' he finally had to shout out over the sound from the chugging diesel. From that point on, Captain Hoxie Rolla realised that he had a student who knew next to nothing about the most famous waterway on the continent, and he turned out to be a genuine mine of information, not merely facts, but that which grows out of day-to-day experience, part and parcel of his fifty-odd years on the river.

Together we watched the Missouri sweep into our path.

'The Nishodse or Big Muddy,' as Hoxie called it. 'Too thick to drink and too thin to plough. Flows all the way from a place called Montana, and Mr. Twain tells us that, together with the Mississippi, it makes four thousand three hundred miles. The longest piece of running water on the earth.'

Secretly, Hoxie would have loved to have been a pilot on a grand paddle steamer back in the days when the river was the life blood between north and south. And as befits such a calling, he knew every dock, every turn in the river and how it had changed since he had last passed this way. And sometimes when fuel was tight, he would steer us right into the middle where the current was strong, shut down the diesel and let us drift right through the evening, a wash of moonlight being our only guide. With him and his first mate, a man called Tourte, taking turns on the watch, I for one enjoyed seeing the sunset slowly sink into the gun-grey light, feeling as if we were slipping back in time. I remember how it reminded me of a Dutch painting I once saw in a picture gallery in Dublin – the colours simple; browns for the land and silvery, green greys for the water.

Sometimes we would drift in silence for hours on end, and it was surprising how much you could see when your eyes grew accustomed to it. At other times we would listen to Tourte play his harmonica, or Hoxie would light up a curious-looking clay pipe and give us a history lesson, a pipe he claimed was made by a people who prospered on the banks of the Ohio long before the time of Christ. I can see him now, carefully cleaning it out before doing the same to himself, hacking up a large gob into "the great cuspidor", as he sometimes referred to the waterway.

'In the year 1542, a Mr. De Soto was the first European to lay eyes on the river.' He spoke quietly, while packing his pipe as his mind ticked on. 'And that was at the same time the great Italian artist Michelangelo was busy trying to keep his Pope happy by painting that chapel in Rome. I would dearly love to behold that wonderful ceiling.'

And then, on a clear cool evening as we neared Saint Louis, we stopped for a short spell, and he took us ashore.

'People say this is a new country, and yet over there was a pyramid larger than anything outside Egypt,' he explained, pointing to a large black mound, silhouetted in the fading light. 'The great city of Cahokia stood on this site over a thousand years ago. Thousands of folks fishin', farmin' and tradin'. Not that different than what we do now... God only knows where their people came from.'

In Saint Louis we took a mooring at one of the smaller piers and unloaded our cargo, everything from second-hand fridges, to potted petunias, to cats in a box. The orders were that the crew was to be back the following afternoon to reload. Hoxie and Tourte hauled me off to their favourite blues haunt and with Tourte being a mix of black, Indian and white blood, I was the only pale face in the place. The music was powerful stuff, and I would have enjoyed more had the drink not gone straight to my head. As for sleep, what little I did manage was spent on the floor of Tourte's place. An apartment house would not be the word for it, more of a wooden timbered warehouse divided up into rooms. He and his girlfriend were in the next one along and by the sounds of it, they didn't get much sleep either. Where Hoxie ended up, I don't know, and I never asked.

The next morning, Tourte's friend made the strongest cup of black coffee that had ever touched my lips, before sending me off in the direction of the music college. I made my way across the unfamiliar city, and I remember how good it felt just to stretch out and walk for a while.

Upon entering the admissions building, I caught sight of my reflection in one of the glass doors, and at the first opportunity I went into a toilet and straightened my shirt collar, brushed down the jacket and tidied my hair. Along the main corridor there were many photographs of past teachers and students and as I was beginning to feel a little nervous and out of place, I noticed a young secretary sitting behind a desk.

'Excuse me,' I interrupted, surprised by my immediate attraction to the shape of her bare arms as they busied themselves.

'If you are here for admissions, it is third on your left,' she said without raising her eyes from the typewriter.

'Ah no. I'm looking for a Mrs. Yeoman.'

'Mrs. Yeoman is no longer with us,' she answered, this time looking up, I think partly out of curiosity at my accent. 'She got married and went to live in Washington. That's Seattle, Washington. Is there anything I can help you with?' she then asked, her formal manner belying a pair of melancholic eyes. And when I brought up the subject of Charles Peccatte, her interest increased.

'You are not from around here?'

'No, Ireland… County Donegal. Do you know it?'

'No, but my great-grandfather on my mother's side came from Ireland… Dublin, I believe,' she explained a little uncomfortably. 'Margaret – that's Mrs. Yeoman – has on occasion spoken of Charles Peccatte… in some reverence, I might add. But he was well before my time.'

'I'm doing a little research on him,' I ventured, asking if she knew of any musical compositions that he might have left to the college. She thought not, in a way that implied consideration. Then, to my surprise, she offered to make sure, that if I was prepared to wait until she finished typing the letter, we could go over to the library.

'I know the place well. One day I will be the librarian,' she added proudly.

In the meantime, I went back along the corridor and looked over the photographs, eventually sighting the caption *MASTERCLASS GIVEN BY CHARLES PECCATTE*. And when I saw the figure peering over the shoulder of a tense-looking piano student, it took some convincing to believe that it was the same man who I had come to know, his disease, the operation and the complications that followed having taken their toll. It was almost as if the jacket and the shoes furnished the final proof, for they looked to be what I was wearing. And to top it off, I swear I could just make out the shiny faceless plate of the Reverso watch as he pointed to some phrase in the music. As I stood there, comparing them to the real McCoy's, her voice suddenly came up from behind.

'You know him?' she asked, quite obviously intrigued by my strange attitude. I had the feeling, right or wrong, that she had been standing there for some time and had intuitively guessed something of my situation.

'I did,' I answered, feeling a rush of sweat from my armpits. 'But he has recently passed away, Miss…?'

'Anna, Anna Kittle,' she replied, holding out her hand, those pained eyes acknowledging my solemn words. I shook it, unable to keep my eyes from straying to her arm, that mysterious portion from the elbow up to the shoulder.

'You did say that he was before your time?'

'Yes, but as I said, Margaret spoke very highly of his playing. And I have a feeling there is a tape of one of his concerts somewhere in the library,' she recalled, looking away at some of the other photos. 'Did you ever hear him play?' she asked, checking her watch.

'Not much. He was not at all well when we met.'

Anna Kittle's declaration that she knew the place well was not an empty boast, for she glided between the aisles with easy confidence, and I got the feeling that the head librarian, a pale, wizened old woman, was a little disturbed by her authoritative manner.

Anna soon dug up a few of Charles's recital programs from high up in one dusty corner and afterwards the tape of him playing a recording which the librarian had claimed did not exist.

'Mrs. Yeoman recorded it at one of his concerts,' Anna explained, sitting me down in one of the listening booths, handing me a set of headphones and efficiently putting on the tape.

The piano cut in like a shaft of sunlight. The notes coming across with no effort, every one clear and exact to some inevitable whole, frictionless links in a rippling chain. Its momentum, its tireless musical invention drew me in, or out, like being cleaned by a heavy summer rain. *J.S. Bach* is what it said on the tape case.

A long, dense applause eventually died to the squeaking of the piano stool as Charles made himself ready for what was to come. And if the previous piece held me still, this brought me to attention, like if I had moved an inch I would have been turned to stone by this white-hot furnace of creation.

When I asked afterwards who had penned it, she answered, 'Brahms, paying homage to George Frederick Handel.'

And I remember how her answer triggered an episode from the Lakeside Hospital. Unable to sleep one night, I laid staring at the ceiling, when suddenly Charles sat up from his bed before screaming out through the dead quiet ward,

'Brahms! Johannes Brahms!' He turned and looked straight at me, his eyes ablaze. 'You have not lived until you have let this man in!' The strange thing was that after that outburst, I slept like a log and the next morning, when I reminded him, he remembered nothing, accusing me of dreaming it all up. Well, that day in this college library he had taught the lesson, for Mr. Brahms had certainly got to me.

One man paying homage to a man paying tribute to another ended with another huge applause and as it died away there were no sounds of people getting up, but rather a complete silence, so quiet that I began to think that there was nothing left on the tape. What I had just heard was more than enough to fill me and yet just as I was about to switch off the machine, a string of bell-like notes rang out. In what must have been an encore, Charles produced something of such subtle simplicity, engendering what I can only describe as a painful beauty, a sense of both loss and gain, all at once. And, as the last chords of this brief expression died away, for some reason the painting in his apartment briefly flashed up in my mind. I had no idea who the composer was and when I put the question to Anna Kittle, she answered, 'Domenico Scarlatti.'

While I sat recovering from this concert, the young woman went scouting off to see if there was any music in Charles's hand amongst the archives. Unfortunately, there was none, and I must have been banking on the possibility, for my disappointment showed, and perhaps she was feeling a little sorry for me when she then asked if I would like some lunch.

We passed by various dormitories before the lawn began to decline towards what at first looked like a tall green hedge.

Anna Kittle swung her arm in an arc and announced, 'Charles Peccatte was responsible for that.'

'For what? This wall of green?'

'Not a wall,' she corrected me, and as we approached, I began to make out a number of openings. 'A maze, Peccatte's Maze. Margaret Yeoman told me that when it became known that he was a gardener of some repute, the powers that be asked him if he would redesign this part of the campus. I don't think they realised what they had let themselves in for, and I'm told that when it was first opened and half of the board of governors got lost, they very nearly voted to rip it out.' We stopped and I counted four openings. 'There are a few ways that lead you back to the beginning, but only one which will take you across to the garden,' she assured me.

I followed her through one of the doors and kept her in sight as we twisted through the green corridors. When I reasoned that the incline, slight as it was, would always indicate which direction to go, she stopped to explain that Charles had built that clue out of the system by subtle landscaping which sometimes reversed the argument – up became down, so to speak. My interruption was enough to bring a worried look across the young woman's face, but after a short backtrack and a further moment of hesitation, she eventually found the single doorway. This in turn led us down some steps and onto a path that gently wound its way through a park or "arboretum", as she referred to it. The variety of trees was impressive, and Anna Kittle was proud in her knowledge, directing my attention to a noble-looking Lebanese cedar, a sequoia of great girth, and a spiky monkey puzzle tree.

This arboretum gradually thinned out into a lawn that brought us to a quiet little street, on the opposite side of which ran a long row of older, terraced apartments.

'They don't pay a great wage here, but they do provide me with a place to stay,' she explained matter-of-factly, which is when I realised that we were not going to the college refectory but back to her place.

By now I was feeling hungry, not having eaten since the day before. She offered me a seat at a small table in an equally small kitchen and proceeded to take out the carcass of a leftover chicken from the refrigerator. We shared it out, piling the bits of dried meat on buttered slices of soft white bread.

'According to Margaret, he didn't have another job to go to when he left,' she recalled, slicing me a piece of chocolate cake. I had to confess to a growing attraction to the woman and while watching her pour out some tea, my attention wandered over her hand, purposeful as it was, on up her forearm, past the elbow to that upper arm, the very same area which I had already avoided more than once.

This image has emerged many times since, and I have come to realise that I have been attracted to this area between shoulder and elbow on people before. But not with the intensity of this occasion, and I could only assume that Anna Kittle's was imbued with some sort of ideal proportion, at least for my eye. Its sculpted shape, the way the outside muscle ran from its attachment in the elbow on up into the shoulder, a continually changing curve that no words of mine could possibly encapsulate. And the manner in which her skin wrapped around these muscles, subtly and continually implying their form. For a moment, in that little room, all the mysteries of existence seemed to be embodied in this small stretch of anatomy, and to try and end my staring, I remember asking her if Charles had been well thought of during his time at the college.

'His recitals have become part of the local folklore,' she answered after a few long moments, those brown eyes betraying a depth that I would have trouble putting into words, almost as if it betrayed the collective experience of more than one life only.

'So why hasn't he become better known, I mean in a wider sense?' I finally asked.

'You know, there are some people like that,' she earnestly claimed. 'There is an exceptionally talented guitarist who I have heard, living not far from here. But he will hardly ever get up on a stage and play. He runs a bicycle shop and teaches a little.'

It seemed a good enough explanation for us both and for a while we ate our cake in silence before I broke it with another question.

'And do you happen to know where Charles was living before coming here?'

A plain "no" was her first response as she played with the chocolate between the talons of her fork. 'Although... now that you mention it...' she eventually went on, her words drawing me to the edge of the hard wooden chair, 'I seem to remember Margaret mentioning something about a mansion in the South. In Georgia, I believe,' she recalled, sliding the last piece of cake onto my plate. 'Here, have this... I like it too much.'

'And do you know if he was ever married?'

'Married?' she echoed, rising from her seat to put the dishes in the sink. She repeated the word once more, as if I had opened up more than just the question at hand. 'I couldn't say.'

It was right about then that the ringing of the campus chapel bell made me flinch, which, as I would come to learn, was a reaction to something much more disturbing. I remember my eyes began to sweat, my mouth went dry, and no amount of tea was going to quench such a drain. For a moment I feared another epileptic attack, so much so that I hastily washed down two pills. And while I did my best to ignore any possible significance, she pretended not to have noticed, or perhaps she was by now conscious of her allotted hour, remarking how the new dean was a stickler for timekeeping. I swivelled the Reverso and glanced at its face, confirming that the barge would set sail in just over an hour and that the walk back would take no more than half that time.

As we parted, I suggested that I would try and write to her with some sort of address, so that if she came up with anything else, she could let me know. I watched her cross the road and disappear between the trees and shrubs – back through that area of the campus that Charles had designed.

Part of me wanted to see Anna Kittle again, yet another was keen to be on my way and during the walk back, my mind wouldn't leave the encounter alone and not for the first time I found myself speaking to the wind.

'Are you mad? Falling for an arm pouring a cup of tea! Is this what it has come to? To take to a person because they have a lovely limb. I mean to say, how many similar arms are there in this city alone? In these very houses which I am passing by! But what an arm!' came another argument. 'And what about those eyes, and her nose!' Now that had definitely bothered me, for if I tried to put that appendage into words it would come out sounding ugly, but it wasn't, for somehow the complexity, the connection of shapes, made perfect sense! To fall in love with a nose. I suppose you could have argued that the appendages were beginning to add up, and beyond noses and arms, and what might lie between her ears, I shuddered to think…

After circling round this argument, I tried to steer my mind away with the realisation that I had failed to find any music, that this search was not going to be a piece of cake.

'Yes, two pieces,' my other voice stubbornly spoke up. 'And good cake it was, too,' wondering if Anna Kittle had baked it herself.

And as I walked on through the unfamiliar setting, Charles's playing returned, the sounds from that tape having drawn me even closer to him – giving me a deeper grasp of his frustrations in the Lakeside and re-stoking my desire to track down the rest of his sonata. Back in the hospital I suspected he could once play well, but never did I imagine the sublime sounds that came from that recording.

During all this mental to-ing and fro-ing, I had somehow taken a wrong turn and got thoroughly lost. To make matters worse, when I asked a young boy the way he sent me off in the wrong direction, or we got our wires crossed, my head again flipping back to the subject of Anna Kittle. Eventually I managed to get my bearings, but with time running out I had to make a run for the river and when I did manage to find the right dock, the barge was gone, or so I thought. I can remember vividly this rush of desperation as I ran along to the next pier, and to my great relief, there it was, Hoxie having moved it for better access to our supplies.

And as my pace slowed and my state of mind relaxed, for some reason that missing slice of my life suddenly loomed up. It had always been strangely uncomfortable, living with something which I had no direct memory of, and for some reason it wasn't getting any easier. *But why just now?* I remember wondering, vaguely suspecting it was not chance. And as I was to learn, it wasn't, for although this diversion to the college failed to offer up the rest of the sonata, it seemed that its possible existence was a link to my lost past, that this appointment with the barge and the ringing of those campus bells were in some way significant. Yet with Hoxie calling for help on board, I could make no more sense of the notion and let it pass.

Our supplies were to be taken to a mine near the town of Herculaneum. Not surprisingly, Hoxie knew a few of the miners, having worked there himself for a year or so.

'Saved enough to buy this old boat,' he explained with pride.

After we had unloaded, his next trip was back upstream, but he was planning to return in three weeks before sailing further south, so I had the choice to either pick up another barge, take to the road, or wait for his return. I decided to wait it out, or rather work it out, down in that mine.

The money was good, so underground I went: a place where you had to learn fast if you were going to survive at all. Not that I admitted it to any of those hardened "dogfuckers", as they used to call each other in rare moments of affection, but to my shame I soon discovered that I feared the dark – that is, real darkness, a total, complete absence of light. It was something I had never consciously thought of before I went underground and on the second day, as a joke, if you please, the lamp man gave me a bum battery, and with pick and shovel in hand, my level boss sent me down some disused bit of tunnel with the order to mend some sloppy section of track. After trudging along for some time my lamp dimmed, flickered, then suddenly failed and I came face-to-face with it. And it would be a lie to claim that it didn't send more than a shiver through me. I suppose it was the totality of it. For even in a dark room or on a cloudy, moonless night, there is still something that shows itself – something, however vague, that implies some sort of change when you move your eyes or swing your head – but not in a mine. Down there, everything is exactly the same. Black isn't even the word for it, for black, at least before this, had some sort of colour. Not here. No shape, nor colour. Nothing at all.

Eventually I groped my way back, but not without a long hesitation for fear that at some point I had managed to get myself turned around and was actually walking the wrong way. I have never been so glad to see again, to get my sight back, for that's what it felt like. Of course, the lamp man put it down to bad luck, but I found out afterwards that it was something they did every now and then to one the new boys – just for a bit of amusement.

To call it a mixed crew of miners was an understatement, not only as regards to the colour of our skin – and believe me, there was every tint in the human race down there – but perhaps even more diverse were the reasons and circumstances for ending up under the earth at all. Some arrived a couple of decades ago, or more, with the intention of making their fortune but had ended up staying – lifers, who I imagined had gradually become shadows of their former selves and for some godforsaken reason could no longer take the sun in large doses. Some were men of substance. I especially remember an Indian level boss from the Sioux tribe, a tall, handsome man who they called Chief Dan. From the moment he addressed me I felt respect, and not something which stemmed from a sense of apprehension or fear, for he carried a love for his life's work and gave me the feeling that the mining of rocks from the bowels of the earth was a dignified profession that demanded a clear and elegant train of thought; the kind of man that a mere hundred years ago would have been a great chief, at home with the vast herds of buffalo on the seemingly limitless Dakota Plains.

But he was an exception, for there were many more with hardly an ounce of respect for themselves, their mates, or the earth which provided their livelihood. And they had come from all over the continent and further. Some were like me, there for one month's pay, while others had set themselves a goal and hardly managed to get their boots dirty before hopping on the next boat. As it happened, one of my contemporaries lasted exactly one day. I never found out what they did to him or maybe his own mind did the job, but I distinctly remember seeing him at the shift's end, eyes fixed on the lift shaft roof, unable to blink until he stepped out into the light of the sun. He dropped his lunch pale, never looked back, and I never saw him again.

And there were nearly as many ambitions as there were men to house them. Some I talked to were on the brink of having enough money stashed away to carry out their dreams – a piece of land in Montana; a motorcycle business in Los Angeles; a trip around the world; a chance to play the markets, on Wall Street and Las Vegas – you name it and he was down there somewhere, drilling, scaling and scooping.

And given the stories that floated around, many had got close to their dream, but in a moment of despair, lost both their head and bank balance in a run of squander and debauchery. The two French Quebec guys who I worked with couldn't save a month's wage if their lives depended upon it. One of them was so deep in hock with the local loan sharks that he would stay underground and work triple shifts just to keep out of sight.

As you would expect, the new boys got the crap jobs, knocking or scaling rock from the stope walls – walls that had just been created from a new explosion, and as a consequence, were riddled with loose ore, chunks that could drop off from the merest vibration and knock you dead. Another less than attractive detail was repairing track for the ore cars. If a car came off and it was seen to be your fault, God help you, for the high-ballers at the mining face were on bonus and on a good run they could double their pay cheque. You didn't want to be the one who screwed up and slowed the train to the ore shaft, where it would be weighed, and their wages calculated.

Throughout that dark month, I never became an object of their disfavour, but an incident just as frightening did bring me up earlier than planned. For some reason a scoop tram, which is in effect a low-slung front-end loader, became jammed between two walls of rock and I, along with one other new boy, got sent down to help out in one of the most notorious bonus stopes. There were strict rules governing the use of time-fuses for setting off an explosive, but when this ate into their bonus, some of the more impatient high-ballers would cut it short. The trouble was, on this particular occasion they neglected to tell us, and if truth be known I very nearly got missed altogether. To say I was blown off my feet would be an exaggeration, but the compression from the blast certainly ushered me along with some force – kind of like when you are riding a bike and a mighty gust of wind suddenly shoves you from behind. I was very relieved to see the sky that day, and the next morning I couldn't bring myself to go back down that mineshaft.

I spent the next few days fishing along the river, and it was a welcome sight to see Hoxie's boat come steaming into port late one afternoon. After unloading the supplies and indulging in a feast of crawdads and beer, we continued chugging our way south towards Cape Girardeau.

That river trip was full of memorable passages, but just now, as I gaze upon the descending terraces of blooming flowers and varied shrubbery, its essence seems summed up in one particular evening. Up until then it had been cool, but on this occasion, as we finished our dinner of bean soup and bread, a warm mist began to settle. With some trepidation, Tourte and another ship hand kept mentioning Tower Rock, an infamous geological formation that pilots seemed to fear.

I remember Hoxie offering to give me a lesson in river reading – the manner in which the water's surface revealed what was under or beyond it; a solid sand bar or bluff reef you could skim close to, if need be, but you never must let the boat pass over it. This was to be distinguished from wind reefs, merely spots of river that the air plays upon. Not an easy thing to judge, especially when the weather is grey and misty. He explained the difference between these and a snag, and of course the buoys, which indicated safe passage. He let me take the wheel for a short while, but it was not something

I enjoyed, for my mind would convince itself that every little apparition had deadly meaning, some lethal obstruction inches under the water that would slit the hull in two.

When Hoxie could see my knuckles turning white, he let one of the others take over and handed me a beer.

'From Saint Louis,' he said, holding up the brown bottle to the fading light. 'Worked in the brewery for a while. That town makes more brew in the time it would take to down this than a man could drink in a lifetime.'

'You've never been off this river?' I asked, eyeing his big brown face reflected in the passing water.

'Took a holiday once. Went up the Missouri as far as Kansas City,' he admitted, taking a long guzzle and turning his gaze onto the darkening shoreline. 'Along here is what is known as The Trail of Tears. Not for the first time, the government of the day broke a treaty and forced the Cherokee to leave their homeland for somewhere further west... back in 1830-somthin' it was. Thousands perished. . . There's been plenty of blood shed along this ole river.'

It had been a long stretch of seeing very few signs of modern life, and during that time I found it easy to imagine what it must have been like back then.

We drank our beers and continued to gaze into the passing trees. And although we did not talk about it, I felt that for both of us, the darkness held some secret which seemed out of our grasp. It was about then that I pulled out those photographs.

'Nice place. Around here, is it?' Hoxie asked, taking another long drink from the tall-necked bottle. I showed him the smudged writing on the back, but he had no ideas. 'If you headin' Georgia way, best you get off near Memphis,' he suggested, turning to the next photo. 'Good lookin' woman, and some garden at that.' The next was of a large wooden house surrounded by a rich variety of trees and shrubs. I didn't think it was worth showing, but he insisted. 'Now that could be anywhere,' he confirmed, briskly finishing his beer and pulling out another from his pocket.

The last image, The Tomb of the Diver, held Hoxie's attention for a long while. He never said anything about it, just stared, the way men of any self-awareness do when their own mortality comes to mind. Something that unexpectedly brings them to their knees – in some, releases their humility, if only to silently acknowledge a moment in time – that indeed (unless they are of the mind that truly believes in the hereafter), to realise, the moment, is all they have. And I suspect with most, there is the nagging sense that on the whole they haven't made as much as they might have with what has passed before them.

'So what brings you into these parts?' was what he eventually asked.

'Oh, a friend said he liked the river,' was my lame reply.

'Yeah, but most just gaze out from the comfort of their automobiles, or high up in one of those air-conditioned tour buses, not ride some workin' boat down this old snake.'

And when I explained that I was inclined to fall asleep on those buses, he smiled broadly. 'Oh yeah… With only your dreams for company.'

As it happened, I had been dreaming an awful lot of late – more images than my daytime mind cared to admit – and as Tourte sat down on deck and began to play his harmonica, Hoxie downed his beer and said his goodnights.

Perhaps it was the drink, mixed with that forlorn eerie

tune, for by then my mind was adrift – thoughts from another time and place, like the varied bits of wood that occasionally slipped passed in the lead-coloured current. I recalled when as boys we used to drop painted sticks into one of the bigger *sruth* that criss-crossed our land. The excitement of seeing them bob and slip along, disappear under a bridge or a piece of winter ice, and to try to stay ahead, to place bets that your colour would be the first to show itself. We would work our way through the valleys and peat bogs, racing to the coast, hoping against hope that we'd keep sight of them until they reached the sea.

Once we stopped to watch an old farmer prodding for bog oak, ancient trees which long ago used to cover the hills. He struggled onto some high ground to scan the frozen grass, spotting where the frost had turned to water, a sign that there could well be a log underneath. His prod, his *bin Maide*, as he called it, would sink down into the peat and when it went too deep, he would grunt and move onto the next. When pleased with what he felt, he threw us a few spades and we dug, and with the help of his son we eventually managed to pull out an ancient log, black as coal and hard as stone.

I recall all of us gazing at the trunk in silence, I expect all wondering about the nature of time, how many generations had come and gone since the tree was alive and growing. The old man smiled and gave us a generous drink of his *Poitin* to send us merrily on our way.

This childhood reflection dissolved to the course at hand… and to doubts. Like what the hell was I doing, wandering through this vast continent on the few words from a sick, half-deranged man with nothing but an odd little cobbled-up will and a few old pictures to carry my hope that there was something to be found! After all, he had travelled plenty and could have composed the other movements anywhere. And given his swings of mood, he could have left them anywhere: on a train through India or dropped them into some smelly Venetian canal in a moment of despair. Was I mad? I had to wonder.

But moments after these doubts had rampaged through, that tape from the college library returned to my mind's ear. Again, I heard the dark majesty of his playing, pictured the refined movement of his good hand on the keyboard of the battered upright piano in the hospital common room, and those brief flickers of energy in his eyes. And his words to himself: *the only thing you have ever really finished.*

I reached into the lower pocket of my new inheritance and pulled out the diary, turning back to those words, *follow the music.* I didn't pretend to understand everything he had let fly from his troubled soul, but I was reminded that I had him to thank for renewing a kind of faith which had all but been extinguished from mine.

By this time, the mist had almost cleared. We slipped past Tower Rock without a hitch and, mad as it sounds, a sense of disappointment seemed to infuse the crew, as if being let off so lightly had left nothing but a gnawing emptiness inside. Hoxie went off to bed, yet I was not for sleeping. The sun dropped as the moon rose, and the great river emerged like a wide ribbon of liquid silver, reaching into a thickened darkness. The sky moved from black indigo through deep blue to many shades of red and orange, and all the while Tourte played on, the shifting sounds of harmonica wailing over the low throb of the lazy chugging diesel.

And as I gazed out into the entrancing scene, my

grandfather came to mind – not the tinker but my father's dad, a fisherman. He lived with us until he died, and I recalled an occasion not long before he passed away. I couldn't have been much more than three, sitting on his knee and running my small white fingers over his forehead, feeling the roughened texture of each wave of skin. He was happy to let his grandson wander over the ancient landscape, my gaze finishing on his watery eyes, these meeting mine with something of a half-smile. And even then, I was aware that the craggy features were a result of pushing a century, that I too would grow to look something like this, if I was lucky enough to make it that far. And with that, I remember trying to wish his wrinkles away.

And with those wrinkles another story floated up, or at least the idea of it. One of the few books I had managed to get through as a young student, and on that evening, perched as I was on the bow of that dark hull, it returned. What was it the man had said? 'Mr. Kerns,' or "Kurdz", 'he dead.' Something like that. Or was it, 'He not dead.'?

Even at the time, to my young mind, it hardly seemed to matter. For, as young as we were, we all knew it wasn't merely a man that the riverboat captain was pursuing, but something that was mirrored in us all. And towards the end of the captain's tale, when he had returned to England's shores, didn't he eventually meet the man's wife? And wasn't there some sort of rumour that he had been a musician? I suppose in a kind of way, back on that gloomy hospital ward, I had met up with my Mr. Kerns or Kurdz or whatever his name was, that somehow he was not done with me, that the dark secret or unfinished business would be my work to unearth.

On that warm evening, the heavy current, like some sort of invisible rope, silently pulled, and me, a mere frightened half-baked mortal, lost, with not a clue of what lay ahead.

Just south of New Madrid, I would never have believed the width of the water had I not seen it with my own eyes. Before entering the state of Tennessee, we tied up near a place called Reelfoot Lake, which had been created during the earthquake of 1811. For those river dwellers back then, the deluge had come true.

As Hoxie put it, 'The fear of God's wrath had filled more churches than any evangelical preacher ever could,' spoken as if he had been there; so convincingly, in fact, that I was happy to accept the impossibility.

Eventually we docked in Memphis, and after unloading, Hoxie decided to stay on for a week or so before heading back up-river. But he kindly had a word with another captain and arranged for me to take a barge further south and before we parted, he showed me around the city, a tour which included the place where the reverend Martin Luther King had met his end. The river trip would conclude as it had begun: with a history lesson. For as we both contemplated the hotel balcony, Hoxie quietly recounted a famous moment from his family's past, of how Abe Rolla, his great-grandfather, had obtained his freedom in an extraordinary way. He'd had gone to bed in a slave state during a prolonged downpour, and that night the great river broke its banks with such a force that by morning it had changed course. He awoke from his bed a free man in a free state.

As Hoxie went on to recount, 'The man had a few drinks to celebrate. He sang in the church the whole of the next day and prayed to the Mississippi forever more.'

As we walked back to the old barge to say our goodbyes, I for some reason mentioned Ship Island, one of the seemingly disconnected facts that Charles had come out with. I was not surprised when Hoxie knew of its existence, but as it happened, it was one of the few places that he hadn't been to. Still, he did recall that this particular piece of land had become separated from the river's present course – a little like his story of Abe, only this time the river had been diverted by an engineering project back in the 1940s. The only other thing he mentioned was that the place had something to do with Mark Twain and although he wouldn't say why, he suggested that I go and have a look.

'It's in the state of Arkansas, down-river from the town of Dyess,' was the last thing he called out to me as his old boat moaned and creaked off its mooring.

When I eventually arrived at this place, the story I got from one of the locals was that in 1858, the steamboat *Pennsylvania* had exploded and foundered on the island's banks. The storekeeper assured me that its remains were still down there and that during one dry summer he had got a glimpse of its rotting carcass. The twist was that the young Sam Clemens was a student pilot on the very same boat, but on that particular run, he had been detained in New Orleans. Not so his brother, however, for he was on board and lost his life – a theme which was not about to leave me in peace – and it all got me wondering whether it had been, in some odd way, the same for Charles Peccatte.

INTO GEORGIA

After the river it was hard to get back on the road, but I soon managed to pick up a ride to Tupelo. From there, I picked my way through Alabama, heading for a place called High Point in Samson County, Georgia, the name that I figured was on the back of the Landray Mansion photograph. When I finally got there, I showed the photos around, but no one had heard of the place.

With hope fading, I went into a bookshop on the main street, and a small black man at the counter assured me that there was no Landray Mansion anywhere near High Point, saying it in a manner which left little room for doubt. Disappointed, I began to browse the bookshelves and, as whenever I did such a thing in such a shop as this, or a library, I soon got the strongest urge to use their conveniences. Afterwards, when I had returned to the front of the shop, the black assistant had been replaced by his sleepy-eyed boss, a huge, very blond man, almost to the point of being an albino. I couldn't have imagined two more different examples of the human race. For some reason I re-presented the photo, but like his helper he showed no glimmer of recognition. As a last resort I turned over the picture.

'It's all smudged,' he announced before I explained my reasoning. 'Then, my boy, it could just as easily be in Lawson County, on the far side of Atlanta,' he suggested, beckoning me to step into his office where a large state map was pinned on the wall, and I watched with intense interest as his big forefinger moved around. 'There!' he exclaimed like a child putting the last bit of a puzzle into place. 'Far Point! Passed through there once. Pleasant enough. Your fancy mansion is surely down there.'

The more I looked at the first word on the back of the photograph, the more I began to think he was right. Certainly, the first letter looked more like an "F", than an "H". So, after a sleepless night in a local hotel, I caught an early bus for Atlanta. But as I rode along through the lush countryside, I had plenty of time to convince myself yet again that this was nothing but a wild goose chase.

Once in the city, I plodded mindlessly through the hustle and bustle, and my spirits were no higher when I boarded another bus destined for Far Point. True to form I slept most of the way, only waking when we ground to a stop in the main street of the town. The jolt had yanked me right out of a dream, or should I say The Dream, with that ominous wave rolling in towards the rock. The only difference was that this time I was on the slippery stone, watching in terror as the frothy water rose around my feet. When a voice called out, 'End of the line,' I woke with such a flinch that I all but knocked the little woman who was beside me off her seat. The sound of shuffling feet began to clue me in on where I was and while still in a stupor, I took my place in the line of passengers as they silently made their way up the aisle and out into the stiflingly hot sun.

Once again, I got out the mansion photos to show to a few passers-by, but the smell of yeasty fresh bread soon enticed me into the Blue Bird Café. The proprietor, a large black woman with a steady eye, produced about the best ham sandwich I have ever eaten and that, along with a cold soda, began to revive my spirits. It was whilst I was making my mind up to go to the local land registry office that the answer literally came out of the air. A teenage girl and her mentally impeded young brother had sat down beside me, and as I was digging into my pockets to pay the bill, I put the dog-eared photos down on the counter. As soon as the boy laid eyes on the picture of the mansion, he called out, 'Landray!' And as his sister began to apologise, he continued as loud as before, 'Pass by her place… most always,' he insisted, his large round eyes bulging with excitement.

His enthusiasm brought the proprietor over. 'That sure looks like the Landray place, all right… or did,' she confirmed. 'The house ain't so impressive nowadays.' When I showed her the photo of the woman in the garden, she gathered it up, putting on her thick rimmed spectacles to study it more closely. 'She don't look quite so impressive now neither.'

'Who is she?' I asked.

'Why, I'm thinking that's Marion Landray,' she claimed. At the mention of Charles Peccatte, her large brow furrowed. 'Now that you mention it, I believe she did have a husband once. But that was before we moved here. Who he was or where he went, I couldn't honestly say.'

As it happened, the proprietor's son, a laconic character with a glass eye and one thumb missing, was about to make a delivery of groceries in the direction of the mansion, so I was duly offered a lift in his pick-up truck, a very old, matt blue machine that seemed as loose as a vehicle could get without drifting apart.

"Hello" was the only greeting that passed between us during the bumpy ride, for when he suddenly pulled over to let me out, he merely nodded up the leafy avenue before grinding the machine into gear and driving away. And as I walked past several magnificent mansions and gleaming limousines, I remember thinking how curious it was that Charles's jacket, shoes and watch could well be returning to his former residence on the person of someone else.

When I did eventually arrive at the Landray property, it was clear that Mrs. Drake, the Blue Bird proprietor, had not exaggerated, its obvious decay being in vivid contrast to the well-kept houses that I had just seen. So much so that I had to take out the photo to make sure it was the same place, for it was not only the wholesale neglect that struck me, but how much the trees had grown, changing the space and scale of everything. And what made the scene even more astonishing was its contrast with nature, for it was springtime and amongst this decay of paint, board and shingle, everything was blossoming into life!

I remember leaning against a large chestnut tree, which in the photo was about half its present size, and watching for any sign of life. But as evening descended, I gave up and walked back to the Blue Bird quarter of town, booking myself into a poky little room at the Greenland Hotel. All I remember of that first night was gazing into my own tired-looking eyes in the cracked shaving mirror, washing down two epileptic pills and falling into a creaky bed.

The next morning, I went back to the Blue Bird and had a much needed breakfast of waffles, bacon, eggs and two large cups of easy drinking coffee. Just as I was finishing, a truck marked *Landray Logging Company* rolled past the front of the café and I couldn't resist asking Mrs. Drake if there was any connection.

'Same family but that's as far as it goes. They been loggers and landowners from way back.'

'Some say Sam Landray has built himself a mansion in the big city,' piped up one of her regulars from behind a newspaper at the next table.

'Some say! Some say a whole lotta bunkum, Henry!' she offered.

Between them they conveyed that when Old Man Landray died, his only son Sam inherited everything but the old mansion. He even fought his sister for that, but in the end, she won out. As Mrs. Drake put it, 'Yea, after nearly a month in court! Inheritance, it can be a nasty business!'

'Not a month, Liza,' her customer chipped in. 'God knows why she fought so hard. I mean, she hasn't exactly kept it up! Half crazy, some say.'

'Some say, Henry, some say,' she repeated while adding up the bill. 'Now, would you like anything else, young man? I have fresh cherry pie. I have pumpkin pie with a touch of cinnamon, topped with thick whipped cream. All to your pleasure.'

I must have forgotten that I had just eaten more in the past half hour than in the previous two days, for I succumbed to a piece of her rich brown pumpkin pie, and she wasn't joking about the thickness of the cream. Halfway through it was getting painful to breathe in, but with her proudly hovering around my table I wouldn't have dared not finish.

After that I walked around the town to try to relieve the pain, eventually working my way out towards the mansion. I took up my position in the welcome shade of the chestnut tree and fell asleep more than once, waking up to find the place just as I had left it, with no sign of any life whatsoever. As Mrs. Drake was to confirm, Marion Landray spent most of her time in Atlanta.

That evening I went to a place called Tubbs's Bar. 'The only joint in town with any *real music*,' as Henry informed me. There were various jazz musicians who took their turn. Some I enjoyed, some feeling more like a run-on sentence. There was a bluesy rock group that turned my head but, be this as it may, I must have had too much to drink, for when I woke up the next morning, I found myself lying on the floor in my hotel room, still dressed, shoes and all.

With one of my notorious head colds coming on, I made the by now familiar walk to the mansion and did so a few more times that week before getting fed up, so much so that after one fruitless stake out, I encouraged a loose slat off the high wooden fence that surrounded the back of the property and stepped through. And what a sight to behold! A virtual jungle of misshapen trees, prickly bramble and monster weeds, crowding out a few patches of diseased lawn which were fighting a losing battle for what little light filtered down. By climbing an ash tree on high ground, I began to make out some kind of previous order – what looked to be a series of terraces dropping down to some huge poplars with the faint sound of a stream somewhere below. The thick growth near the stream all but covered what appeared to be a little domed temple, but after almost falling out of the tree, I took my leave, for to explore much further I would have needed a machete.

By the next morning my head cold had truly taken over and, unwilling to face another walk to the mansion, I remained in the dingy little room all day, rising only to relive myself in the rusty sink. It was one of those monster-driven sleeps, where I have a fear that dawn will never come, yet when the grey light finally found its way under the broken roll-blind, I wished it hadn't, feeling as flat and groggy as ever.

THE RECLUSE

By the next day I was feeling a little better, and after a coffee at the Blue Bird I repeated the walk, this time varying the route. The superstitious would have claimed that this change made the difference, for, to my surprise, an old Ford sedan was parked in the drive. It was a rusty heap that was in keeping with the mansion's flaking façade and at complete odds with the gleaming limos parked elsewhere along the leafy avenue. Taking up my usual position against the chestnut tree, I didn't have long to wait before someone passed by one of the upstairs windows. A little nervous and with my head feeling like a beehive, I approached the entrance and rang the bell. When this had no effect I tried the heavy brass knocker, each bang leaving flakes of peeling white paint on my hand and shoes. After a long wait I heard the dull rumbling of footsteps on stairs and the door slowly opened, a jaded, suspicious face staring out from a darkened corridor.

'Yes? What is it that you require?' came a deeply suspicious question.

The figure stepped forward from the raised entrance and

a distrustful eye entered a piece of sunlight, staring down upon me and causing my bout of nerves to grow worse.

'Ah… good day. You must be Mrs. – or Miss – Landray?' I managed to stutter out.

'And what if I am?' she replied, visibly offended by my runny nose, by my very presence. 'If you are peddling insurance, or wanting a handout for some crooked charity, you have knocked on the wrong door.'

And then when I said that I knew Charles, she didn't so much as raise an eyebrow.

'No doubt many people have had the privilege,' she uttered in some contempt, while all the time I was wondering how this spiteful face before me could possibly be the smiling, intelligent image in the photograph – as I was to learn, a woman some twenty years younger than her former teacher and husband.

I took a stunted breath and went on ineptly, mumbling something about the last time I saw him, and my use of the term "fortnight" (which wasn't nearly true) only seemed to confuse her even more. Unimpressed, she began to shut the door.

'Charles… he has passed away!' I finally blurted out.

Only then was there a change in that closed face, albeit for the briefest of moments. After I explained where and how he had died, we stood in silence before she enquired whether I was one of his students.

'In a manner of speaking,' I answered, explaining something about how we both loved gardens, and 'Would I be right in saying that he created one here?'

Judging by her reaction, this subject seemed even more repellent than insurance or charity, suggesting that if horticulture was my interest there was a botanical garden in the centre of town. She then coldly thanked me for conveying the news, and before I knew it the heavy door was firmly shut in my face.

On that warm spring afternoon when Marion Landray had left me on her doorstep, the last thing I remember was walking down the drive and turning to look back towards the mansion, considering whether to return and start again. On reflection, it was almost certainly the fact that I had let my pills run out. I suppose the head cold and the heat could have both played a part, or maybe it was also something else, some sort of ill-defined despair which had befallen me.

Whatever it was, once more I found myself back in hospital, having passed out from another epileptic attack. When I came around, for a moment, before I registered the nurses' Georgian drawls, I suspected I was back in the Lakeside Hospital in Chicago, that, in fact, this voyage south had been nothing but some strange dream. My head had taken one hell of a bash when I hit the pavement, and it was pounding sore under the turban-like bandage.

The doctor who admitted me was not quite sure who he was treating, having gone through my inherited jacket and found Sean Gallagher's wallet but Charles Peccatte's diary. Sometime later that day – or was it the next? – one of the nurses said that they had received a phone call from someone asking after me. I assumed (wrongly, as it turned out) that it had to be Marion Landray, the notion giving me the belief, the hope, that there still might be a drop of warm blood in her veins.

Over the next few days, I read every book on gardening that was in the hospital library, my plan being to pay that woman another visit. Although the medics wanted me to stay on for another day, I was itching to go, Charles's money having long since disappeared, and what mining pay I still had was also running low.

I settled the bill, checked back into the Greenland Hotel and took the walk out to the mansion. As usual there was nobody there, so I prized off that loose fence slat and had another look over the broken down terraces. I'd borrowed a set of shears from Mrs. Drake that enabled me to cut things back enough to squeeze along some of the old paths. Between each successive terrace there was a set of stone steps, some passable, others not. Across one set, there were two yews that had begun life on opposite sides and over the years had grown together, and further down a lilac had seeded itself right in the middle of a cracked step. Cutting around this, I managed to wade down through the underbrush to the bottom of the property where the stream gurgled past. From here the house didn't look in such a bad state, and I could also see that the best place to get a view of the garden was from its balcony, but that would only be possible from inside.

The sorry state of the place brought home nature's ways; how, especially in such a warm, damp climate, gardening must be a process of constant care. It was obvious that *it* did not give a damn for man's borders or sense of proportion. *Still*, I remember thinking, *the place must have been most impressive in its day.*

After exploring the bottom of the property, the stream, the lawn, which had turned to soft spongy moss, and the ornamental pond a few terraces up, which was clogged with a bright green sludge, I found myself following the various rose plants that wound their way through the broken trelliswork. The area was so thick with surrounding trees and shrubs that the damp air was dead still, which is perhaps why most of the plants were covered with disease and parasites.

And it was about then, as I was crouching down to take a closer look at a blackened, yellow-flowered rose bush, that she spoke.

'It may be sick, but I don't believe it is any business of yours!' came the strong southern accent, languid and confident in its tone. And when I turned to look up, there she was, silhouetted against the sky. I apologised for entering her property uninvited but this she ignored, accusing me of scheming to sue her for my accident on her driveway.

'I can just imagine some upstart of a lawyer, some ambulance chaser,' she began to speculate.

As I tried in vain to assure her that there was no such lawyer, I began to feel dizzy, knelt down and for some reason turned my attention back to the sick rose.

'I don't see it as my business to attend to nature's shortcomings,' she argued, seeming to relish the disease. But as the sweat began to ooze from underneath my bandage, she crouched down beside me. 'It is only the beginning of May and already the sun is stifling.' Her hard tone softening, if only slightly. And looking into her dark eyes, I thought I caught the briefest glimpse of something resembling concern. 'I was going to have some tea... now that you are here,' she suggested.

With the first step into the parlour, the cool air began to lift the sweat from my brow. The room was dark, much darker than it need be, as all the shutters except those covering the French windows that led onto the balcony were firmly shut. Before disappearing to make the tea, she offered me a seat, the form of the chair indistinct along with the rest of the furniture, having all been covered with dust sheets. My eyes took some time to adjust to the poorly lit space but having done so it became plain that it was a beautiful room, or had been in its day. Despite its neglected state, there were hints of its former glory. The peeling, faded wallpaper revealed numerous rectangular patterns where paintings used to hang, and the beautiful wooden floor looked bare without the oriental carpets which I imagined it must have once possessed. A grand piano remained, with its curved shape dominating one end of the room, its black legs protruding below the massive white sheet.

It felt like the sunlight was trying to get in, only succeeding where a shutter no longer hung straight or where it partly penetrated the dusty lace curtains on the French windows. With a cool stillness about the air, it was as if the room was perpetually in mourning.

I could hear the odd noise from Marion Landray's preparations, echoing along the corridor from a few rooms away. Eventually she entered, tray in hand, seeming a little more relaxed now and within this subdued light I was struck by the grace of her movements. It made me think that she was not as old as my first impression, her darkened, dare I say, vengeful soul having sped the clock, disguising an otherwise attractive air. Without a word she pulled off the sheet from a little round table next to me, placed the tall cup down and proceeded to take a seat.

'So, Mr. Gallagher…' she began, taking a long drink, the nape of her neck catching a stronger source of light, 'you obviously have a natural concern for gardens.'

I corrected her pronunciation of my name (the "gh"

being soft) and immediately her whole being went tense as I carried on as if it was not important.

'Gardens, yes. My mother took great pride in hers and I used to give her a hand. But it isn't nearly the size of this one.'

'And where exactly would that be?' she asked, her tone now a little forced.

'Ireland. County Donegal. On the edge of the sea,' I answered after taking a drink.

'Is something wrong?' she enquired, equally sensitive to the slightest change in my expression.

'Ah, no. I was just expecting the tea to be hot.'

'You mean to say that you have never had iced tea?'

'Cold tea on occasion. But not iced… This is a beautiful room,' I continued, carrying on in the face of her silence. 'I was told that someone called through to the hospital?'

'Was a beautiful room,' she answered, ignoring my enquiry. 'As you can plainly see, the paintings are all gone,' she went on in a slow, musical way, which had the effect of disguising the meaning of her words, almost as if I was listening to a foreign tongue.

After another few more sips of iced tea, I asked if she played the piano, to which came an emphatic, 'No.' But even then, I knew it meant quite the opposite. Charles seemed to be hovering in the air, but for some reason I dared not mention him. Our awkward silences were beginning to add up and as I peered through a crack of light between the lace and the French windows, she came to my rescue – or got her revenge.

'I shouldn't strain your neck, Mr. Gallagher,' she insisted, over-stressing the pronunciation. 'Please, go, have yourself a look.'

In the sparsely furnished room, my footsteps echoed across the wooden floor.

'If the name bothers you, you can try Mooncoin,' I suggested.

'Mooncoin?'

'Yes. My father used to call me that. The story goes it was the place where I was conceived.'

Only after a hard pull did the doors give way, letting the light flood in. I stepped out onto the generous balcony, while the woman remained inside, still as a stone. Leaning on the metal railing while sipping the iced tea, I gazed over the descending terraces, suddenly realising that the photo – the one of her in the garden – had been taken from the very same spot. Quickly I slipped it out of my inside coat pocket and began to compare the two scenes, the stark differences between them making what lay before me seem even more pitiful. Some trees had grown way out of proportion to what was around them, while others had fallen down, half buried or entangled in one another. Various shrubs were quite obviously not in the plan, several having taken root in the middle of the main path that joined up the terraces. The formal hedges had grown all out of proportion and it was no longer even possible to stand where Marion had posed for the photo, a huge laurel hedge having long since pushed its way into the space.

When she eventually decided to come out into the light, I secretly slid the picture back into my pocket. As it happened, her thoughts were still on our previous subject.

'Used to?' she asked before seeing the answer in my eyes, for even though it had happened so long ago, I could barely talk about his death. Possibly because it was always there, like a trick played by some ancient malevolent god.

'I can well see how that laurel used to be. A neatly trimmed hedge, much lower and curving around one end of the rose garden,' I offered instead. 'And a low wall, I can imagine there must be one somewhere amongst that yew.' She said nothing so I pressed on. 'And along that boundary wall, I can see an espaliered apple tree... or a peach.'

'Why, yes.' Marion Landray finally spoke. 'A peach tree used to grow there. It produced large, splendid white fruit. One year it caught a blight so bad it never recovered,' she confirmed with a mere hint of regret, before quickly devouring this touch of weakness and returning to the parlour. 'Would you care for a little more... cold tea?' she asked, though her thoughts seemed elsewhere.

Her resentment was almost palpable, a dislike of life and, by implication, of Charles, which seemed to have no end. And yet this seemed like a kind of perverted passion, which for some reason I felt might contain quite the opposite, and as I stood there surveying the neglected garden, I wondered how big a stone it would take to disturb her dark depths.

I returned to the subdued light of the parlour, and it was then that I mentioned the idea of restoring the garden: mending the broken walls, separating the weeds from the specimens and so forth. This produced a lengthy silence, as if she was waiting for such an outrageous suggestion to just drift away. A world that she had consistently neglected, even intentionally starved, was threatening to seep back through the cracks of imprisoned memory. She may have been unhappy, most probably preferred it that way, but up until that moment, at least she had some sort of handle on her singular life. And yet even *she* could not let the suggestion just pass.

'Presumably you see yourself as a restorer of such a world? To create order out of chaos, as my husband used to say,' came her intimidating return, tinged with such bitterness as to make me wonder what in hell I was letting myself in for. And no doubt the woman sensed my dilemma and went on, 'If your land turns barren, Mr. Gallagher... sterile.'

I gulped my tea at her "gh", for some reason recalling the feeling when you dip your toe into a bath of such extreme temperature that for a moment you are not sure if it is boiling or freezing. In my discomfort I walked over to the covered piano and ran my hand along its curved lines. For some reason, Grandad came to mind; more specifically, the last time we were together, near some rocks looking out to sea.

'My grandfather once told me that if the music does not fall under the fingers, put the fiddle down and *Port a' beil*, taking heed of what lies beneath the notes, beneath even the words... pretty or solemn as they might be.'

'*Port a' beil*?' she questioned.

'Lilting out a tune with your mouth. A kind of song without words.'

'And this tune, this song, was it anything in particular?' she wanted to know.

'Yes... and no,' was an honest reply. 'We were on the *tra* at the time.'

'The *tra*?'

'The strand... the beach, the tide lapping around our feet.'

'Lilting... Singing without words?'

'Yes,' I confirmed, the notion leaving a deep impression upon her, offering a look that suggested I turn explanation into deed. So I did, commencing with a tune that my mother would sometimes sing, in her garden, when she was in good spirits, or for that matter, low in her heart.

And after I'd finished and my mind had returned from Bloody Foreland, I could feel Marion Landray's eyes on me, looking long and hard before she stepped back out onto the balcony. The recollection and the song had released something in me, loosened my bones and tongue. I too left the soft light of the parlour to gaze at her, the strong afternoon sun presenting few details.

'I have watched nature have her way for the better part of a decade. Why in damnation should I stop its inevitable victory?' the silhouette asked.

Again, I had no answer, but strangely enough I felt like getting closer to the woman – an inexplicable attraction mixed with the desire to make us both feel more uncomfortable than we already were. So I stepped up near to her, and whether it was the effects of the music-making or something else, when I gazed down upon the horticultural chaos it began to transform in my eye. No doubt the photograph had helped, but it was more than that – like time sliding back. The sun was warm and with my tongue relaxed (almost as if I'd had a few drinks), I had the desire to express this feeling, without really knowing what would come out.

'Now, that I couldn't say,' I began, 'but I can well imagine how these terraces used to be during an afternoon such as this. Warm... wonderfully warm,' I quietly continued, looking up into the sky, that handsome woman in the photograph coming to mind, and then bending over the railings to where the house met the first terrace. 'Can you see her leaving the kitchen door? Making her way onto the newly mown grass, under the arch of yellow-flowered laburnum... Passing the rhododendrons, she stops, to rest... To fall asleep on the wooden bench... To dream in the cool blue shade of the magnolia.' And by then her conflicts were palpable and I nudged a little closer. 'And as the sun begins to free the shadows, she wakes, perhaps from a dream. Pulls her hair back and wanders on, through the rose garden, its scent perfumed, almost overly so... The bees and the like are going about their business, while the reflections on the lily pond catch her eye. Approaching, she gazes into its watery passages, up along its muddy edges, dry and cracked... Continuing on past the ancient yew, she descends towards the mossy lawn. Each step cooler, a little darker, submerging into a sweet smell of vanilla, the fragrance spreading... sifting up from the deep pink blossoms of oleander.'

We had been having our share of awkward silences over the past hour, and after my extravagant imagining, we stood still in the sun and let time slide for a while, left to gaze at the array of tangled shrubs, broken walls and overgrown paths. Eventually her response came.

'I am afraid I have an appointment to keep,' she offered coolly. 'So... if you have finished your... tea.'

I seem to recall repeating my desire to "make a stab at creating order out of chaos", and as she ushered me into the front hallway and opened the large front door, I remember looking down at the flakes of paint left on the doorstep from my previous visit. I thought she was going to let me go without another word, yet as I stepped outside, she dryly asked where I was staying.

'The Greenland,' I answered, her eyes by then fixed on the far distance.

The next morning, after a dream-ridden night, I made

my way to the Blue Bird Café. I remember taking a seat in one of the familiar booths and without even placing an order, Mrs. Drake brought over a generous breakfast.

'I take it you have met Madam Landray,' she predicted, setting down the plate of eggs, bacon and pancakes.

'Yes, I found the woman.'

'Then no doubt you'll need your strength,' she professed, pouring out some maple syrup onto the fluffy stack.

After a few days of lounging around, I decided to "take the walk", as I had begun to call it. The old Ford was not there, but instead of turning back, I slipped into the garden and with hardly a conscious thought, I found a broken rusty trowel and began to clear the weeds from one of the rose beds. If I had been in a more considered state of mind, it would have looked a daunting task, but I got blindly stuck in, gradually working up to a kind of fever pitch. It had recently rained, so most of the weeds came out clean, that is, except for one tall, broad-leafed variety which had a root that seemed to go down forever. As I was to learn, these were impressive survivors, the tiniest speck of remaining root soon turning into a new plant. In fact, since they produced little bunches of pretty blue flowers, I had the idea of taking advantage of their tenacity and creating a whole flower bed of them. But before putting such rashness into practice, I came to realise that they would eventually take over the whole place.

After a couple of hours of picking and scraping, I had managed to expose a sizable patch of the flowerbed and as evening descended, I departed, my fingernails jammed black from the loamy soil.

RESTORATION

A few days later I was woken by a ringing telephone, the hotel receptionist nervously exclaiming that there was someone to see me. Still half asleep, I suggested he send whoever it was up to my room, to which he replied that the woman was waiting impatiently in her car. She had obviously put the fear of God into him, and I pulled on my trousers, dragged a comb across my head and hurried down the stairs.

Marion Landray drove off before my door was even shut and, apart from her silence, there was immediately something odd – not odd so much as evident, in that she handled that old car like it was part of her, like there was some mysterious directness between her hands, the steering wheel, the tyres and the road. Without a word, she turned on the radio and we listened to the weather report before she fiddled with the knob and came up with some classical music. Nothing at all passed between us until we rolled through the front gates of the mansion, then it poured from her lips like rising water from a sluice gate.

'...And I want to make it clear from the beginning, I cannot afford to pay you a great deal. Room and board and fifteen dollars a week would be all. And I am not always here, which means you will be on your own a good part of the time,' she announced, removing her sunglasses, the detail sticking in my mind as it was one of the darkest days I can remember. 'Well, Mr. Gallagher, do you still have the stomach to do battle with this weed-infested ground?'

I don't really know how long I took to answer, but I do remember wondering to myself, *who the hell was the fellow who said, "You better be careful, you just might get what you ask for."?* I also remember looking into her large eyes, at the ample contour between eyebrow and lid, before nodding in affirmation.

Her tour started with the garden library, two long rows of dust-covered books in one of the back hallways, before moving into the kitchen, and after showing me the cookery essentials, she suddenly took an interest in my headscarf (as Mrs. Drake had come to call it), which by this time was looking pretty scruffy.

'I thought this was meant to come off. Here, sit down,' she said. I did as I was told and she began to unwrap the bandage, her hands moving with a clear and elegant purpose. 'So… you don't mind being on your own?' she enquired as the last of the wrapping came free.

'Oh… I've had worse company.'

'I'll show you your room,' she said, stepping out of the kitchen before I had time to stand.

The room was on the top floor, airy and large, with plenty of light, a comfortable bed and a bird's-eye view of my new place of work – a far cry from the dingy little hole at the Greenland.

True to her word, Marion Landray wasn't around much

and as my work got underway, I soon rediscovered every muscle in my body. Yet despite a fortnight's effort, I made but a mere dent in the overall situation. I began by making a mental schedule of how long each job should take, but that idea soon fell by the way. When weeding, I often wasn't sure what to pull out and what to leave. The library would then be consulted, and if that didn't solve the problem, for the most part I would just let the plant be, or put it in a pot and deal with it later. This sounds like good sense but I'm sure more than one prize specimen met its death along the way.

But getting rid of weeds was just the tip of the iceberg. For one thing, the soil had become very poor and needed nourishment. In a sense I was lucky in having a large heap of compost that had been left to rot down, undisturbed for the better part of a decade. The rub was that it sat close to the stream, which meant every load had to be barrowed up, sometimes as much as five levels. This was made possible by placing a plank over each set of steps for the barrow to ride over – that is, once I had cleared the steps of unwanted plants.

A session of runs was hard, sweaty work, but the truth was I kind of enjoyed it. After about a half a dozen runs my shoulders and calves began to hurt, especially by the time I had reached the top terrace, which, to make matters worse, had a few extra steps and less space to manoeuvre. If I was feeling strong and made it to a dozen runs, I rewarded the workman with a prize – a bottle of beer and the chance to cool off in the stream, and by that time the cold flowing water felt good, even in the pouring rain.

But the compost was not enough, for in many places the soil was thin and poor, and it was during a prolonged dozing spell on the other side of the stream that the remedy came to me. In fact, the solution occurred as a dull scratching sound: a large mole going about its business directly under my ear. In short, this patch of meadow with its rich black topsoil was gradually being brought to the surface. I remember looking up "mole" in the encyclopaedia to discover that it ate over half of its body weight every day, a fact that I soon began to believe as I gathered up a daily load of earth from the fresh little hills.

There wasn't a bridge over the stream but there were the remnants of some consciously placed stones, and after repairing this watery path I began making my way back and forth with a couple of buckets. I lost my balance over the course more than once, falling head over heels into the stream, but in general the plan worked well, on average collecting two to three barrow loads a day. The only thing the little animals removed was the earthworms, and once I had the scheme up and running, it was a matter of making a mix of soil and compost in a barrow before taking it on up into the garden.

After another week or so, part of the top terrace was beginning to look something like Charles had intended and when Marion Landray eventually returned, I had the desire to show her my progress.

'Didn't they teach you to knock in County Donegal?' came her irritated response when I looked in through her study door.

'Not when it is already open,' was the answer that came out of my mouth.

It was not a good start and when I asked her where she had been, she looked at me as if to say it was none of my business.

'Atlanta. And at present, I am rather tired. So if you don't mind, close the door behind you.'

That evening (after our separate meals), there was an ill-defined tension in the air, a mutual estrangement. She was obviously accustomed to being on her own, and I was beginning to get used to the same. I remember taking the dust sheet off the grand piano and tinkering around with a few Irish tunes, ones I knew well. At home I would often go to our little upright and play around, this sometimes producing a new idea on the fiddle but on this occasion any such attempts did little to lighten the air.

'Do you need anything for the garden?' she eventually asked, without even looking up from her magazine.

After she had cut me short earlier in the day, I didn't much feel like being straightforward with her. Some sort of odd verbal dance was developing between us – questions left hanging, perhaps to be picked up later, ideas thrown up only to die in the air or be trampled over by some other notion. A curious game of hide and seek, give and take, wrestling with each other's presence and pride, with on occasion a small dose of generosity to keep something in play.

'A fine piano, but it could use a tuning. What do you exactly do in Atlanta?' I had to ask.

'I work in a bank.'

'In a bank?' I could hardly imagine her in such a place and by the way she answered I felt it was not a job she had been doing very long.

'And before that?' I presumed.

'If you must know, I taught music… at a private school,' she reluctantly answered.

'So why did you leave?'

'Rich, spoiled, undisciplined children. I lost my patience with one particularly obnoxious and untalented little brat.'

'You said you didn't play the piano.'

'I don't!' came the quick reply.

And I bet she is good, I thought, returning to her original question. 'I could use a new lawnmower. Yours burns more oil than petrol and it's becoming impossible to start.'

'That costs. You are going to have to wait for that.'

'Then how about a new rake? Half the teeth are missing on it. Some manure, and cement and sand to rebuild the walls. And fertiliser for the lawns.'

'I will arrange an account with Dawson's Hardware. But mind, I want to know exactly what you spend!'

I turned my attention back to the keyboard, experimenting with a few more tunes, before trying out Charles's piece – the passages that I could remember by heart. By this time she had returned to her magazine, but it wasn't long before the music started to make an impression. Out of the corner of my eye, I could see her begin to stir uncomfortably, yet she refrained from enquiring and for some reason I didn't seem ready to offer any explanation.

I kept working on the terraces and they gave me plenty of variety. Once I had managed to cut back the rampant undergrowth to expose the various stone walls, it became obvious that their condition was even worse than I had feared. One of the problems was that the roots of overgrown trees often caused a section of wall to bulge, so badly that in a few places it had toppled down onto the next terrace. In such cases I had to choose between cutting away some of the tree's root structure with the hope that it would survive, or taking it out altogether. Sometimes I could rebuild the wall to its original state, whilst at other times it was all I could do to get the stones back in place. Having laid bricks before helped, but even so, my first attempts left a lot to be desired. Some of the more extreme bulges on the taller walls actually looked attractive, in effect a kind of slowly moving sculpture, a ticking time bomb that one day will inevitably topple to the ground.

There were plenty of overgrown shrubs and trees to get to grips with. The two yew trees that were planted on either side of a terrace stairway had grown into one another. At first, I thought they would have to be chopped out altogether, but in the end, I made a feature out of it by giving them one flat face and rounding the rest, like two half globes which had been split apart by a descending stairway. According to my topiary book, with proper feeding they would recover, although the north-sided face would presumably take longer.

The blessed roses were another matter. Some seemed to have gone into permanent hibernation, while others had gone rampant, winding their way into trees and stonework. The sick ones I fed and sprayed, and the wild ones I cut back. When I really got into the job, I realised that Charles (or was it Marion?) had created a series of arches, which for the most part had lost all their form. With these I was at a loss to know what to cut and what to leave, and it seemed that most would have to be grubbed out and new ones put in their place.

With the lawns, I began by raking out the moss, pulling out the weeds and throwing down some fertiliser. During these weeks Marion would come and go, on one occasion only stopping for a few hours before vanishing again.

Sometime after that, our encounters began to loosen up a little, then something wild happened. The underlying engine was Charles's music, which up until then I hadn't mentioned. I kept intending to, but days turned into weeks, which became almost two months, and still I had not broached the subject.

I certainly had not given up on finding the remaining parts of the sonata, and this came to a head after another dream-ridden night. I remember waking up in a sweat and looking out of the window into an absolute downpour. Not just hard rain, but torrential sheets of water and whether it had anything to do with my dream, I can't say, but the sonata issue suddenly took on great urgency.

Feeling restless, I got up with the purpose of telling Marion straight away, but she was not around. I managed to unlock her bedroom door with the idea of finding the key to a tall cupboard in the parlour. On occasion I had seen her lock things away in it, and sure enough there were several keys in the bottom drawer of her dresser.

One of these did the job and as I pulled open the large oak doors, a lace tablecloth fell from the top shelf. I needed a stool to return it and tucked away at the back of the shelf I found a violin case, and with a quickening pulse, I placed it carefully on the piano. Tied to its stout brass handle was a yellowed paper label that read *Jean.* Charles's sleep-talk suddenly came to mind: *Jean! ...Jean! You out there?* Various questions followed: Who was Jean? Why was his fiddle here? And where was *out there*?

With no answers, I opened the lid to reveal a beautiful violin, one that seemed as old as my Panormo, its dark orange varnish glowing amidst the cradle of green velvet which lined the case. It looked to be in pretty good condition, bar an old crack near the chin rest. The A string was broken and although there was an extra one tucked away in the case pocket, I didn't much feel like disturbing the sound of the rain, so I laid the instrument back in the case and returned it to the shelf.

Lower down in the cupboard there was a large photo album. Various pictures filled its pages: the garden in different stages of development and the house looking in much better trim. Others showed friends and guests during happier times. One in particular sticks in my mind, of a younger Marion, sitting at the piano in a fetching dark dress. She was striking, with a crowd of smartly dressed admirers gathered around her, all in high spirits. Yet amongst this revelry, she looked to be utterly submersed in the music at hand. The photograph centred on her purposeful hands so clearly that a knowledgeable pianist might even be able to tell what she was playing. Could it have been some of Charles's music? Maybe even one of the earlier movements of the sonata? Almost certainly Charles was behind the lens, for in all of the pictures there was not one of him.

Looking further, I found various newspaper clippings – a praising review of Marion as a music student, and one of a recital given by Charles. In this there was a picture of him at the piano, his hands by his sides, as if he had just finished a long, taxing piece, and when I came across two stacks of music shoved in the corner of one of the lower drawers, my pulse quickened again. Leafing through I found Schubert, Mozart, Beethoven, Rachmaninov and of course Brahms, but nothing by Charles Peccatte.

With all of the memorabilia spread out on the piano, I suddenly felt hungry and went off to make myself some breakfast, taking it out onto the balcony under the big sun umbrella. It was then, while listening to the pelting rain and planning my next work project in the garden, that all hell broke loose, or should I say, walked in. For when I turned around, there stood Marion, soaking wet, with a look of murder in her eyes.

'Oh… with the rain coming down so hard, I didn't hear you arrive,' was all I could muster up.

'Plain to see! And what, may I ask, is the meaning of this?' she demanded, holding up the key to the cupboard.

Tongue tied, I walked to the piano and pointed to her newspaper clipping.

'It appears from this that you are worth hearing.'

'I beg your pardon!'

'The Rachmaninov.'

'That's Rachmaninov, Mr. Gallagher!' she exclaimed, hardening both the "ch" and the "g". 'And did it take you long to find this?' she asked, pushing the key into my face. We looked at each other squarely before she turned away. 'I think you'd better get your things and leave!'

What few apologies I attempted fell on deaf ears and as I walked out, I remember thinking that it was the best way out for her, that she really couldn't handle any such change in her life.

'Too damned mean!' I remember saying to myself, my behaviour being just the excuse that she was looking for! Maybe I was fed up too, needing a break from the place. All work and no play…

I found myself walking into town, moping around in one of the seedier bars before getting something to eat at the Blue Bird. Mrs. Drake wasn't there that day, which was just as well as I was in no mood for conversation. Come evening, it was still pouring down and I wandered over to Tubbs's Bar, the cold clammy rain soaking me through once again, and feeling like pneumonia was a mere stunted breath away, I entered to the sound of a jazz band, the only source of light centred on the stage at one end of the smoke-filled room.

Being a Saturday, the place was packed, and a three-piece ensemble was in full flow. I squeezed in at the bar and ordered a beer, and whether it was my wet sponge appearance or the fact that I hadn't had a bath for several days, my neighbours soon began to give me a wide berth.

I like a lot of different music – well, if not like, at least have some idea what people get out of it. Perhaps it was just my sour state, but to me this group had little sense of variety, like a run-on sentence leading nowhere in particular, other than the end of their session. By the time they had stopped for a break I had put away two beers, maybe three, and I was in the kind of mood where five would have gone down with little effect, angry as I was with myself, that woman, the world! Yet at the same time, feeling so dreadfully alive all over.

As the band was being slapped on the back and given drinks, I left the bar and made my way up on stage and sat down at the piano. I began by trying out Charles's music, and whether it was my bad technique or my numerous memory lapses, the crowd was, to say the least, not very appreciative.

'Hey! Wet head! Give us a break!' came the first unambiguous call from a drunken young Yankee who looked unhappy before I had entered his life.

Marion's reaction was still rattling around in my head, like a pinball with no way out.

'You fool! Why the hell haven't you given her the music?' I cursed. 'She could play it. I know she could!'

'Hey, boy! She might be able to, but you can't!' came the next heckler, sitting but a few tables away.

I looked over to a big man, dressed in an impeccable blue suit with a yellow rose in his lapel. He was with his wife. She must have been his wife, for if she had been wearing the same blue suit and had his head of slicked-back greasy hair, she could have passed as his brother. She looked embarrassed: whether it was for the idiot at the piano or the one next to her, I wasn't sure. He downed a large bourbon and just when he was about to continue his speech, my first fan piped up again.

'What does this dumb fuck take us for?' was I think the way he put it.

The problem was, I couldn't honestly answer him, and the hostility only stoked my desire to keep on playing. A waitress who was cleaning one of the clean tables caught my attention, her expression screaming out from her tired eyes – *I've seen all this before, so could you not make my life any harder than it already is?* This, along with my growing intolerance at my own incompetence, was enough to finally bring me to a grinding halt. I remember thinking how I didn't so much mind making a fool out of myself, but there was no excuse for doing it to Charles. But whether it was blind pride or just a feeling of sheer frustration, when I got up off the stool, I stared right back at my first heckler, and by now the place was taking notice. He was not about to avert my challenge and as I walked towards him, I very nearly knocked over a fiddle that happened to be perched on a stool. Thinking back, it almost certainly saved me from a broken nose, and maybe worse.

'Holy Christ! A one-man band!' came the blue suit's next insult as he downed another bourbon and nodded to the waitress for a refill.

As I put the bow to the strings and those fifths began to converge, nearly everyone in the place looked up from their conversations. The question was, would I get the chance to play before an empty glass came hurtling my way? It was *Paddy in the Park* that began to calm the natives; even the two guys in the front table with itchy knuckles and too much bourbon in their eyes began to relax. The regulars holding up the bar swung round to reveal their red noses, while the fiddler in the band rose to his feet, crossing his arms and staring out suspiciously at the stranger who had hijacked his instrument. As for me, I was gradually but surely beginning to sail, any effects of the beer vanishing as the rhythmical winds (one of my grandad's terms) began to talk to the fingers, reminding them it was not a shovel, or a garden fork, but an ebony fingerboard. Following this came *The Stage*, a hornpipe that was especially appreciated in the pubs of Chicago.

By conclusion of the hornpipe my joints were well-oiled, and my mind was slipping into a kind of trance by the time I entered a little slip called *The Fairy Jig*, another tune which Grandad swore was handed down from the good little folk. And it was during this that I began to miss the sound of a bodhrán and took to improvising on a foot drum. By then I couldn't exactly say what the crowd was hearing, but after the hornpipe *The Rights of Man*, the reels started flowing thick and fast: *Miss Patterson's Slipper*, *The Dispute at the Crossroads* and no doubt a few others which got mixed in for good measure. This got them tapping their feet and a few were even dancing in the aisles.

God knows how long it all ran, for after that I made it up as I went along, eventually slowing it all down with *My*

Father's Lament, during which, as I improvised within the faerie's rhythms, I could have sworn I tasted the salty sea on my lips. Certainly, by this time those southerners had got a generous portion of Irish folklore, and when I eventually laid down that fiddle and walked out, there was not a heckler to be heard above the applause. I say no one spoke, but when I looked back before taking my leave, one black guy was still dancing up a storm, and I'm sure that nice man in the blue suit called out, 'Hey, Irish! How about I buy you a drink?' Walking in the rain felt just fine.

RALLENTANDO E SMORZANDO

Given that I had rashly thrown my key into the garden before storming off, I had to scale the balcony and jimmy open the French windows. I was hungry but so tired that after only half a bowl of Cheerios, I went off to bed. Why I kept buying that ridiculous food I'll never know.

I woke a few hours later. The rain had stopped and without its constant rhythm on the roof, I felt strangely empty. But as I rolled over and tried to go back to sleep, a faint but curious odour began to take my notice. Marion never wore any perfume but did exude a curious scent when she was tense or excited. The closest thing I can compare it to is refried spaghetti and meatballs, and although this sounds unpleasant, I must admit to liking the smell. As she admitted much later, she was glad to come upon the half-eaten bowl of cereal and my nakedness on the unmade bed.

With this scent in the air, sleep became impossible, so I tiptoed down the stairway and gently opened her bedroom door. I sat down on a cushioned stool beside her bed and as my eyes adjusted to the darkness, she gradually appeared, the bedcovers moving to the rhythm of her breathing. Plenty passed through my mind, not that I can remember much detail now. One thing is for sure, I very nearly got in beside her. Her face was relaxed and still, with a beauty which seemed all the greater, given what I knew of her inner conflicts. As for me, my intentions swung between caution and abandonment – able to talk myself into either scenario. In the end I tiptoed out, and even now I'm not sure why the pendulum stopped at that.

The next morning, I was up early with the clear notion to cook a serious breakfast – orange juice, omelette, bacon, toast, and proper ground coffee. The cheese omelette even had fresh flat-leafed parsley cut into it, our first taste from the garden. I suppose it was partly to make amends and she took it well, very surprised that I could even cook.

But this was a mere prelude to the important decision: to show her the music, something that I should have done earlier.

'And what, may I ask, are you doing?' she enquired as I placed the manuscript on the piano stand.

'Come have a closer look. Come, sit down!'

'You know I do not play this monster,' she still claimed. 'So, just kindly tell me what this is?'

Marion hated to be cajoled into anything, and while it is not in my nature to demand things from people, I made an exception and insisted that she sit down. With twisted expression she finally lowered herself onto the piano stool.

'This is Charles's writing… and where did you find this?'

'He gave it to me.'

'Gave it to you? Now, why would he do that?'

'To be honest, I'm not completely sure… As I told you,

we were in the hospital together... in Chicago... I was with him towards the end.'

'This is not easy.' She grimaced, looking deeper into the score.

'He and I attempted it. Play a little. Come on... I know you can,' I prodded.

In turn, she insisted that I had no idea how well she could play and quite suddenly closed the book and began to stand up. My instinct was to hold her down, so I placed my hands on her shoulders. It was the first time I had ever touched her, felt her frame through the fine cashmere, one of the few luxuries she allowed herself. She pressed hard but then gradually relented and one of our long moments of silence ensued. What went through her mind before slowly re-opening the cover, I do not know, but eventually she put her hands on the keys and began. Halfway down the page she fluffed a passage and ground to an abrupt halt.

'Come now! Don't be so short! It's marked tranquillo!' I exclaimed, recalling Charles's aggravated instructions to me.

'I *can* read!' she barked, with a look of someone being held captive.

I waited while she stared at the notes, her nostrils flaring slightly to the rhythm of her strong but controlled breathing. This time she meant business, and when her hands finally came down on the keys it was different, immediately making sense as she played beautifully for a good three or four pages.

'That was good! Very good!' I walked around to see her face, still completely absorbed. 'Now, the question is... where is the rest of it?'

'The rest of it?' she repeated in surprise, finally raising her eyes off the page.

'Yes, surely this is not the only movement,' I proposed, sensing her scepticism. 'I feel it! There must be more!'

'You feel it?' she questioned dubiously.

'Yes. And besides… Charles said as much.'

'Did he now? And did the great man say where it was?' she enquired with more than a hint of doubt.

When I admitted he did not, her mistrust was plainly evident, and at this I pulled out his diary from my jacket pocket and handed it to her.

'This was his… as was this jacket and the shoes.'

Astonished, Marion looked over the garments, as if somehow feeling she should have known. Slowly, she opened the worn cover and began to leaf through the diary.

'There, stop,' I suggested as she came to some musical notation. 'Now, this phrase is not in the manuscript. And as you can see, it finishes with a double bar line… presumably the end of something.'

'*Rallentando e smorzando*… slowly extinguishing,' she read out.

'Yes. Now, following on he writes three bars, which are the same as the beginning of the manuscript.'

'So you believe that the first part is the end of a previous movement? But it might just as well be a theme he didn't use! Or from another composition altogether. And besides, why in heaven's name should he do such a thing?'

I tried to explain my theory to her – that the two movements were many years apart and he was reminding himself of how the previous had ended before putting down his ideas for the next.

'Yes… a hell of a long time between two movements,' she argued.

'Well, Beethoven's first sketches of the ninth symphony were laid down some ten years before it came to be,' I countered. 'And what about Richard Wagner? I think it was his opera *Parsifal*… conceived in the summer of 1845 but not completed until… until, I think, sometime in the 1880s – over thirty years!'

This does not sound like Sean Gallagher to me! Her eyes replied as she held back a wry smile.

'I was reading through some of his books on music…'

'His books? Where?'

'In his flat, his apartment… in Chicago.'

'Just happened upon the key, did you?' she jibed before returning to the diary, leafing past his drawing of the dwarf rhododendron and then coming upon the strange little will, the declaration that he had put together in the hospital, less than a day before he died. Marion stared in disbelief, resentment tinged with derision creeping across her face. '… *All my belongings… follow the music*,' she read out loud. 'The romantic old fool! So, this is the reason you came here? To take what you think is yours!' she accused.

'I wanted to find the rest of the music…'

'Well I can tell you now, this place is all mine!' And before I could say another word, she went on. 'And even in the state of Georgia, I don't believe there is any law that states that a husband can give his wife away!'

'Wife? You mean to say, you never divorced?'

'Why, I could rip this up right now and you wouldn't have a leg to stand on!' she cried in wild contempt, her face turning red as her lips went white.

After this outburst I didn't feel much like reassuring her that I had no designs on the property.

'And what other surprises does this little book contain?' she wanted to know.

I watched her hungrily search through the writing, turning the pages while her breathing quickened and slowed, eventually closing the little book and dropping her eyes.

'The man was always writing things down! Strange things! On backs of envelopes, on shopping lists!' she complained, while circling around the piano before stopping in front of me, some part of her already trying desperately to explain something away.

I waited for *the something*, expecting some protestation to exit those lips, but instead she turned in silence and walked out onto the balcony and into the warm evening air. I waited a few moments before following her out, all the time wondering what I might be unleashing.

'You were trouble. I could see that,' she continued, half to herself, as if some crack inside had finally given way under the weight of a long-carried burden. 'Strange... it was his watch on your wrist on that first day that sent a shiver through me.'

'The watch?' I repeated, stepping closer to her and holding out my wrist to reveal the Jaeger-LeCoultre Reverso.

'Yes,' she confirmed, glancing at it briefly before staring back out into the vista. 'The garden is looking better. You, like some messenger from the back of beyond... oh yeah, I realised it the first moment I laid eyes on you,' she admitted before pausing for thought. 'The summerhouse.'

'Pardon me?'

'Try the summerhouse.'

'The summerhouse?'

'Yes. That's what I said. On the other side of the stream, buried in that bluff of trees... It was his place,' Marion concluded.

THE SUMMERHOUSE

I wasted little time – made a second pot of coffee, cleared up the breakfast dishes, and key in hand, made my way through the garden, across the stream, over the small field and into the dark bluff of mature beech trees and evergreens. Even on a bright day there is not much light in there, and after about fifty yards I came to a small clearing.

At first, I saw no sign of any human habitation, but after coming upon a deep, clear pond, I noticed the corner of the summerhouse; not a house but a shack, the brown-grey structure being all but swallowed up by various forms of foliage. The entrance was covered over, and after struggling through I came to the mossy door. Not surprisingly, its lock was rusted tight and try as I did it wouldn't budge. Relenting, I went back to the house for my secateurs and an oilcan, and upon returning it took a lot of pumping and rattling before the lock gradually eased.

When the handle did finally turn, the door wasn't about to give up its secrets easily, swollen stiff from years of winter damp. It withstood more than a few hefty shoves before noisily giving way, grinding and buckling the mouldy cork tiles which had curled up on the other side.

My first impression was the smell of mildew as I groped along one wall, stumbling over various objects towards the vague outline of a window. It opened with a hard pull, although its shutters would hardly budge, caught outside on the sagging branch of a tree. By rocking one shutter, the other eventually swung out and a shaft of sunlight cut into the abandoned room. It was a sight: cobwebs stringing through the air to cover hundreds of books that were everywhere – not only lining the walls but piled up on the floor. A willow branch wound thick with ivy had succeeded in getting in through a hole in the wall and continued on up to escape through a small, broken skylight.

As my eyes adjusted, other objects began to take form. Along one wall was a collection of seventy-eights, ancient discs that must have dated back to the beginning of sound recording. An old valve amplifier and a stoutly engineered turntable sat side by side on a shelf with the loudspeakers positioned in two corners of the room: purposeful-looking, large, flattish objects covered with copper screening. At first, I took them to be electric heaters.

The more I gazed along the bookshelves, the more I began to realise that the range and depth of subject matter was even greater than in the Chicago apartment. An old desk stood in the middle so that when Charles had sat down behind it, he would have had a good view of the pond. But no chance of that now, for there must have been twenty yards of scrub between the window and the water. The desktop was in red leather, in one area almost bleached white from the effects of the afternoon sun. I got the strong impression that Charles had spent many long hours here: reading, thinking, working out plans for the garden. Perhaps even composing, as in one darkened corner there was an upright piano. I pressed a key and not surprisingly it stuck down with a dull thud.

Sitting at the desk, I began to feel quite nervous, suddenly realising that the rest of the music might be within reach. I opened one of its drawers to see a couple of old Leica cameras, high-quality machines that were well-used. Underneath, there was a bundle of black and white photographs wrapped in garden twine. Untying them, it quickly became apparent that they were all on the same subject: Europe in the Second World War. There were many powerful images: frightened young men waiting to go into battle, quite a few of a beach, strewn with equipment and corpses. On the back of one of these was written, *Omaha, D-Day plus one.* As I was to discover, this was the code name for a four-mile stretch of the Normandy French coast, and on the 6th of June 1944, it seems that over three thousand young men had met their deaths when the sea-borne attack came close to failing. All of this brought back the well-thumbed travel section in the Chicago apartment, where there had been at least half a dozen books on this same area of France. There was little doubt that Charles had revisited it.

The pile of photographs presented too many potent images to take in: chaotic moments in the heat of battle; tanks on the offensive; tanks burning; dead soldiers on the roadsides, both German and Allied; towns all but levelled, their histories gutted. When I'd seen enough, I began filing them back as they had been arranged, but I was compelled to pause on one image in particular, a strangely haunting scene of a landing craft filled with soldiers disappearing into misty waters. Just visible in the background was a thin strip of beach with dark cliffs towering on one side, and while contemplating this, his words drifted back into my mind: *your father? …Died at sea? …Cliffs. Death out of concrete cliffs.*

And as I peered into that deadly coast which concealed a waiting enemy that would take the lives of many of those men, the strange smell returned to my nostrils, the smell that came before my fit in front of the mansion. Suddenly I realised that I hadn't taken my pills. Where were they? Up in the bathroom? No, on my bedside table…

'Stop panicking and calm down!' I ordered, closing my eyes and trying to hold the scent at bay. But it came again, along with *that bloody rock!* And my mind kept sliding… And I let it go, back to *that* afternoon…

* * *

The boy is waiting, impatient for his mother to emerge from the house; the air light; the sun shining. He turns his face into the sea breeze.

'Sean! You've forgotten your cap!' she calls to her son, arm outstretched.

'But Mother, it's a fine afternoon.'

'It will cool out there when the sun goes down. You'll want it then,' she insists, handing it over. 'Now, you've plenty of time… but still, don't be tarrying too long!'

He makes his way down to the beach, always fascinated by what the surf brings in. Bits of wood, shells… once he had found a broken oar. Another time, after a big storm, a scythe entangled in a piece of fishing net. But now his keen young eye catches the curves of a small voluted shell – yet this one is different, fossilised in stone, uncannily heavy in the hand. It reminds him of the scroll on his grandad's violin, being so shaped, golden brown with its edges rubbed smooth from years of use. Young Sean reasons that since shells have been around much longer than even old violins, it is surely where the maker got his idea. He puts it in his pocket and walks on towards the fishing pier.

Further along, the boy taunts the waves. A little game he often plays: waiting for the white edge of foam to slide to within an inch of his foot before making a run for it. Inevitably one catches him. It wouldn't be a real game if they didn't wet his feet…

He admits to being in two minds about boarding the boat; likes watching the little fleet go out; likes it even more to see it return, to see what his dad has taken from the sea. But being onboard, actually moving through the waves, that was something different. His father had assured him that he would get used to it, but that day was yet to come.

Feet soaked, he continues along the wide curving strand. The wind is rising, and a big gust sends his cap sailing off, rolling and bouncing across the rippled sand. He hesitates before fetching it, ordering it to stop as if it had ears, but to his dismay the cap is still flipping and rolling when it disappears over a cairn of small flat stones. And when Sean scrambles to the top, there she is on the other side, standing still, as calm as can be. He had never seen her before… or maybe once, from afar.

'Hello, Sean! What a wind! And how it moves them clouds!' the girl announces.

He looks up. They are gathering speed.

'And how do you know my name?'

'Written here, on the inside,' she claims, revealing his cap from behind her back.

'Yea… Give it here, please,' he insists, meeting her shifting, glittering eyes.

'I am Flood, Dearbhla Flood,' she announces as they both stand in silence, transfixed on each other. 'I've learnt a new dance! And today my feet feel so fast! You must fiddle them for me?'

And how the devil does she know I play the fiddle? he wonders to himself. He looks along the coast, but the pier is out of sight, still some way around the arching strand.

'Not now… I'm off with my dad, on a fishing run.'

'An evening run! How thrilling!' she cries, looking out to sea. 'The weather is turning. Come! It'll take no time. And I'll bet you anything, anything in the world, I can out-foot your fingers!'

The boy senses her smile disguises a more serious intent and without knowing why, it both frightens and draws him in.

'I doubt that,' he boasts. 'And as you can plainly see, I've no fiddle.'

'And what of that? There's one on the wall,' she counters, pointing to a little cottage, a place Sean had not noticed being occupied before. 'Come on, Sean! Any wish you want… come on! Let's wish and then play!' And at this, she closes her eyes while he watches the wind lift and whirl her auburn hair, struck by the smooth pearly skin that hugs her temple, high cheek bone and nape. Then, as quick as she had closed them, her bright blue eyes spring open. 'There, I'm done. It's time! Come on!'

Dearbhla Flood offers his cap but as he takes it, she won't let go. And with a surprising strength he is pulled towards the cottage, a broken-down affair, half covered in a blackthorn bush – a sign, young Sean recalls from his grandad, that the faeries are about. He is torn between his inexplicable attraction to the girl and the purpose of his trip, to help his father on a proper fishing run.

Inside, little Dearbhla brings down a fiddle and bow off the white-washed wall, placing it in his hands without looking him in the eye, as if already preoccupied by what she is about to do. As he tunes it up, she carefully steps in front of the hearth and takes a position on a large flagstone, worn deeply from generations of revelry.

'Ready? You've got to warm me up… starting slow.'

Her orders leaving the boy motionless. No matter. She stands still as the stone, and then softly begins to lilt, slowly beginning to move her feet, feet in nail-bottomed shoes that at once make the stone start to ring. Sean tries to begin but his hands are cold as ice from messing around in the sea. He stops to warm his fingers, rubbing them hard on his woolly shirt while all the time growing more fascinated by her building rhythms, each change announced by the ringing of the stone.

Sean starts again and after weathering a few rough patches, they slowly begin to come together. But it is not long before she raises the pace and as they work up a head of steam, she screams out while glaring at the stone, into the stone… through the stone.

'Rise! Rise up! It is time! Rise up!'

Ever so gradually she brings on the pace, egging Sean on, sparks now flying from her small, black-booted feet. And by now the boy is awash with the rhythms, happy to follow her steps, at times even pushing forward to give a lead. She returns his call with strong polished footwork, yet he is struck that there is more than mere polish. That she possesses an uncanny rhythm there is no doubt, talking to it with her form, hanging back, passing through with an inventiveness that ignores exact repetition.

Certainly her stamina seems unquenchable, at one point going into a kind of Highland, looking across with a broad smile, like for all the world there is someone beside her. But the apparition seems to vanish with her grin, and she changes step as if moving betwixt two crossed swords; so real, her steps so precise, that for a moment Sean swears he too sees the glittering steels. And by now the boy is infectious with it. What rhythmical rules each abide are stretched and questioned at every turn, the two becoming lost in a strange musical conversation, aware of nothing but the splendid manifold of sound and movement.

But still Dearbhla Flood continues to stoke the fire, forever raising the pace, forcing the boy's hand to play faster and ever faster. And as the momentum pushes on even higher, his bow tip suddenly catches a string with a terrible crunch, the fiddle very nearly slipping from his hands. Yet still she carries on, shouting with glee, ringing the stone with such a force as to all but drown out the church bells as they count out the hour... the mark for the fleet to set sail.

'Where has time gone?' Sean calls out in disbelief, setting the fiddle down and making for the doorway as the chimes die away.

'But Sean... Sean! My wish. You've not heard my wish! And yours? What of your wish?' is the last thing she screams as he disappears over the cairn.

* * *

'Lunch is ready!' were the words that made me flinch. 'Is something the matter?' Marion asked, standing in the doorway, seemingly unwilling to step over the threshold. The look on my face obviously betrayed more than mere surprise, for I could still hear the banshee's feet ringing that clinkerstone, the great slab being suspended above a dark hollowed space: a resonating chamber traditionally containing the skull and bone of an ox or sheep in order to further enhance its sonorous quality. But as I sat there covered in sweat, my fingertips feeling tender from the wild recollection, I had to wonder whose bones Dearbhla Flood was calling to rise on that day. And yet as her ringing steps faded, so too the rest of the memory.

'Lunch?' I repeated to a now empty doorway, realising that this was the first time Marion had ever prepared a meal for me. But before going up to the house, I looked again at the little grey photograph: the floating metal boat filled with metal helmets, under each one a frightened young man. And I also had to wonder what was still in store for young Sean as I tied up the photos and put them back in the drawer. Along with the lost memory, the smell had vanished, and a chill had come over me, the drying sweat sticky on my chest and armpits. It felt good to get out of there, to walk into the warm sunshine.

Marion cooked simply and had a way of making food taste good. This time she had even brought up some old wine from the cellar and as we sat down and she poured out the drink, her eyes asked only one question.

'Have you found any music?'

Omitting my recollection, I began by exulting over the quantity of books.

'Charles could never pass a bookstore without going in,' she interrupted, showing for the first time a sliver of affection for her husband. 'He even had me looking for editions which he didn't have. More beans?'

'No, thanks,' I answered but she served me anyway. Fresh broad beans covered in salty butter, and all the while those war photos kept looming into my mind's eye.

'So, what did Charles do in the war?'

'In the army. He went to Europe... as many did,' she answered with reticence.

'And the photos?'

'Photos?'

'Yes, I found a bundle from the war.'

'He was always interested in photography. More beans?' she preferred to ask, shovelling the last of them onto my plate.

Despite the good wine, our lunch that day finished on a loud silence. The kind that gets worse if you venture into small talk, something which we seemed unable to do.

A GIFT

The next morning when I came into the parlour, Marion was standing on the balcony, and even from across the room I could tell she was in a broody mood.

'What are your plans today?' she called.

'I'm thinking of digging up the old apple tree. It's half rotten and past its best.'

'Yes, it doesn't bear much fruit. And what it does is sour and tough as leather. Give it the chop, why don't you,' she agreed with a disturbing verve. 'This place is too large… perhaps I'll sell up.'

'What? After you fought so hard to keep it?' I baited, recalling Mrs. Drake's gossip.

'And what do you know about it?' she demanded, turning into the parlour and staring right at me.

'Oh, people talk,' I offered, making for the doorway.

'People talk! Gossip is this town's middle name! Mooncoin, wait!' she then insisted. And as I stopped and turned around, she just stood there in pregnant silence before changing the subject, her look softening. 'When I was young, our family used to go to the races. Make a day of it.

As was customary, we would lose more than win. But every once in a while, I'd feel a sure bet coming on, so I'd tell Sam, my brother, and he would run off and place the bet.'

'Yes?' I probed, wondering what in God's name she was getting at.

'Father would want to know how I could be so sure... but I could never explain,' she continued, looking everywhere but in my direction.

'And why are you telling me this?' I finally had to ask.

'I haven't had this feeling since I was a girl. But this morning I woke up with it.' At this, she reached into her pocket and pulled out a key – *the key*. 'I'm sure you recognise this,' she insisted, again looking straight at me with those intense eyes, eyes that were becoming almost beautiful to me. She dropped it into my hand. 'Go on, open it up... top shelf!'

I did as she wanted, bringing down the violin case and putting it on the piano, doing my best to look as if it was the first time I'd ever set eyes on it.

'Please, go ahead and open it,' she insisted as I re-read the yellowed paper label which dangled from the brass handle. 'Yes. Charles's younger brother... he died in the war,' she admitted in a manner which suggested that there was more to his death than this plain fact. I opened the case and pulled out the violin. 'As you said, people talk in this little town. But as with all gossip, truth can become somewhat embellished, especially when it concerns someone's failings... or fame.'

'My luck with fiddles has not been too good,' was my excuse, suspecting that she had got wind of my night of exuberance at Tubbs's Bar.

'Oh, luck can change,' she insisted, taking out the bow

and handing it to me. 'And if that will of Charles's is to be taken seriously, this is more yours than mine.'

'A pity, the A string is broken,' came my next excuse, which did nothing to put her off, retrieving an extra string from the case and holding it in front of my nose. 'And how often do these sure bets of yours come off?' I then put to her.

She pretended not to hear, and with the string in place I began to try to shift the pegs, which, like almost everything else in this house, had grown stiff from lack of use.

'The bow needs rosin,' I complained, and yet she was handing me the lump almost before I had finished the sentence.

As was plain by then, I was not in the mood for making music and Marion was certainly enjoying the chance to get her own back on me for forcing her to play the piano. After fluffing a few attempts, I huffed and began to put the instrument back in its case.

'Come now, don't be so short! Your fingers are just a little hard from all the gardening,' came a jibe of revenge.

It took a while to get the violin in tune and even then, it soon shifted out. Yet almost immediately I could tell it was a good box. Of course, it needed waking up, playing-in to bring out its best, but it felt like it had something to give, a core to the sound that invited me to search for more. Not that I have had the chance to play very many, but the only other one which spoke like this was my Panormo, embodying great depth and a generosity of voice. I could feel the sound reflecting, generating from the back outwards, yet at the same time, it was not about to give of itself too easily, as if there were layers of colour underneath, sound worlds which the player would have to dig out and grow to understand.

It didn't take that long before this quality began to win me over, and I caught a glimpse of Marion's eyebrows rising up in mild surprise when things began to come together. I started in earnest with Grandad's lament and my initial reticence soon gave way to a mood of experimentation, using a few of the more familiar tunes as a kind of jumping board to gradually build and weave a fabric of improvised sound. On these rare occasions, I have no conscious idea of what I'm approaching, although the journey has some odd sense of direction, of rightness... almost as if it is being created, yet has always been there, all at once.

From that day on, Marion's attitude changed towards me. A little more respect, with a little less formality, and over the next few weeks I started to play regularly, something which I had felt I might never do again.

ARBEIT MACHT FREI

The summerhouse became a magnet, and when I wasn't outside, prying off the ivy and cutting back the encroaching foliage, I was inside, dipping into its secrets. One day, I discovered some plans for the garden rolled up in a cardboard tube. There were several sheets on which Charles had put down his ideas, in part centred around some ancient yews. And not only had he meticulously laid out the structure of the terraces, but also what each flowerbed was to contain.

By then I knew the garden's structure all too well and it was interesting to see exactly how he had envisioned it. And from that point, where possible, I began to restore his vision, replacing the numerous specimens which had failed to survive, things like a *Cornus controversa* and a huge leafed *Catalpa*, which when I had come upon them were diseased and barely hanging on, unrecognisable from the illustrations in one of the garden books. As Marion later admitted, the *Cornus*, or the wedding cake tree, was planted to celebrate their great day. Of course, getting any money out of her to replace them was another matter, but after much badgering she usually relented.

Like in the Chicago apartment, I spent hours rummaging amongst the books and reading, all the time hoping that either the music would turn up, or at least a clue to its existence. One day, when I was getting up out of the desk chair, its cushion, and with it a key, fell to the floor. This key fit one of the drawers that I had assumed was stuck. There was no music inside, but something just as interesting: a dozen or more diaries, going right back to Charles's student days in music college. They were full of anecdotes about his life, thoughts on things he was reading, and dotted throughout, solutions regarding a piece that he was playing at the time, such as a better fingering for a particularly difficult passage or an idea regarding why a certain tempo should be just so.

In one of them, the following was written:

May 6, 1964. The Yakushimanum has settled just fine. And along with the Camellia, the new bed looks better than I would have hoped. Even Dad would have approved.

And upon reading this, one of Charles's sleep-talks from the hospital surfaced in my mind: *"Zeke to Pep's... On Fifteen... Yaku... Yakushima,"* I remembered him slurring out in the semi darkness. I continued on:

October 12, 1964 – Marion is pregnant and seems happy. As for me, the second movement has returned. Plaguing me. I will have to sit down and make another attempt. To be honest I'm more than a little frightened of it. God knows where it will lead.

And judging by his numerous admissions that followed, things were not going well. For one thing, he seemed to be neglecting his recital work, and then this:

December 4 – I've been battling on with it, but I can no longer concentrate, haven't been able to do so for over a week now. We argue plenty. Never used to. Mostly about nothing. And she has stopped playing, and I miss that. Things that seemed solid are turning to dust, and there seems nothing either of us can do about it. Our language, no longer what it was. Perhaps I will go away for a while.

And towards the end of this diary, in a hand which betrayed a man increasingly unsure and disturbed.

January 21, 1965 – Marion is out of hospital, looking bruised but okay. But not the baby. Jean, that would have been his name.

So, what had happened to her, I had to wonder? And her baby, who was to take the name of Charles's brother? Despite his difficulties, here was proof that the music was being forged, and not the verbal ramblings of a sick man, but all down in black and white. And once more, Marion must have known about it. But did he actually finish it? And if so, God forbid, had she destroyed it?

For the next few days, I kept dipping into his diaries, and it wasn't long before I came across a connection in one of the wartime entries:

June 5, 1944 – England, with the 29th Infantry. It is

hard for us to believe it is summer, the weather has been so dreadful. But the Armada is finally on its way. Who would have guessed I'd be returning to the country of my ancestors during such unpropitious days. The reality of war is seeping in. You can read it in our eyes.

June 6 – Off the coast of Normandy. The Continent awaits us. We can hear the aerial bombardment. The waters are rough, and it has been a long trying ride. Many are seasick and would give anything to set foot on dry land. I shudder to contemplate what it will be like in the assault transports.

And then this long entry:

June 8 – Normandy, Near St. Laurent. We are in a nightmare. No words can begin to make sense of it. Jean and I were to be on the same assault transport, but we got split up. We exchanged watches. He always knew I liked his. His transport slipped away, disappeared into the grey choppy seas, towards the dunes and rocks which concealed our enemy.

I couldn't help but look at my wrist, at the very same watch that had been passed between the brothers on such a poignant, ominous occasion. I read on.

When my transport finally got moving, and we got closer to shore, it became apparent that there was no movement up the dunes. Something was terribly wrong. Before this, back in England, we knew that we weren't all going to make it, but in the heaving craft with the heavy enemy fire growing stronger, the possibility became real, became inevitable. No amount of training could have prepared us for this. Too much for many and I couldn't get Jean off my mind. Maybe that wasn't such a bad thing.

They dumped us far too early and even before the landing door came down, the machine gun and cannon fire grew brutal, tearing to get in at us, and as the door lowered it did, the impact overwhelming. Insane. Fish in a barrel. I was determined to stay alive, if only to find my brother, but it was all down to luck.

There was nowhere to go, a dozen or so in front of me. Men who I had got to know, grown to like. Death came in. I don't know how I got out. Must have fallen, or was I shoved off the side?

Sergeant Wells was ahead of me, and he was dead before the door was down. I hit the freezing water and went under. When I surfaced, I was part of the monstrous killing ground. Men, boys, floating in the rising tide, whole transports black and burning. My first step out of the water was onto a corpse, or part of one. But the gunfire was too fierce, and I slid back in and began to work my way along the tank barriers.

Every time I saw a body, be it dead or alive, I looked for the face of Jean. And all the while the enemy kept up a relentless barrage, pinning us in the water. Some were drowning in the rising tide, too much weight on their backs. I swam towards someone who had got caught up in some barbed wire. I think it was

Bob Johnson, one of the medics. As I edged my way towards him, he panicked and set off a mine. When the air cleared, Johnson was gone.

For a time, some gunman had me in his sights and I was very lucky not to have gone down. Working along the beach I searched in vain for Jean. Death still flailing from the dunes and the rocks above. The tide insistent. Pushing, always pushing.

June 9 – Not much more than half of my platoon has survived. From what I can gather, Jean's was hit hard, and no one has seen him. No one has seen my brother.

I got out the photographs again. If I had merely come across one or two, they would not have been quite so poignant, but looking through them in sequence and after reading Charles's words, it became another matter. It was seeing the men change, from relatively carefree, to bored, to eyes full of anxiety and fear. Then later, different eyes, brutalised, stunned for having witnessed, having taken part in, such ridiculous carnage.

On a few occasions, his comments would refer to a particular image. I remember one of a German sniper in a church bell tower. In the diary, Charles admonishes himself for being pinned down without his rifle. He couldn't resist taking a photograph, I assume at considerable risk. But for me, the assault transport seemed to embody it all, the same picture which a few days previously had echoed the death of my father and triggered off part of my lost past. All the helmeted soldiers had their eyes fixed towards the deadly shoreline – all except one, who was glancing back towards the lens. Of course, I had no proof, and given the dire conditions there was little detail to his features, but I couldn't help thinking that this was the last moment the two brothers saw each other, that Charles had shouted out "Jean!" in order to turn his brother's head, and more than twenty years later had with the same call woken me up in the Lakeside Hospital.

There seemed little doubt that Charles had taken the photo in the knowledge that he might never see him again and, as it happened, his worst fears were born out. Had fate kept them together, maybe he would have kept his brother alive. But from what I have seen and read, it seems just as likely that he would have died alongside him.

I set down the photos and stayed with the war years, albeit in a later diary, his southern drawl filling my ears as I read on.

April 28, 1945 – Southern Germany. I was ordered to take my camera, load up with film and head towards Munich. There are plenty of crazy rumours floating around, but this time the reality outstripped them all. Walking into a place called Dachau. Hell, back home, it is nothing but a word.

This followed:

April 30 – In freeing these pathetic souls, you'd think that as liberators we would feel, for the lack of a better word, good. But we do not. This place has a way of implicating you. As if the guilt of man, from the moment he stood upright, permeates all.

*May 1 – Not but an hour ago I caught sight of an inmate
who in my hopeless state I took for my brother. For one
brief moment I was sure it was Jean. I told myself, kept
telling myself, that there was no way he could be here.
But my mind wouldn't let go. As it turned out, the man
was French.*

There were very few photographs of Charles's time in
Dachau. I suspect he could not bring himself to point the
camera. But there was one close shot of the entrance to the
camp which seemed to sum up the absurd horror of it all.
Above the iron gates, the sign read *Arbeit Macht Frei – Work
Brings Freedom.*

On the following pages his feelings had turned to music.
Maybe words had become inadequate, and this was the only
language which held out some sort of relief.

BROKEN GLOBE

Marion was going through a change. Showing her the music had become a kind of watershed. Late one afternoon, not long after I had chopped down the old apple tree, I was walking up from one of the lower terraces when I came across her pulling out some weeds from one of the flowerbeds. An area I had yet to tackle, and which had little left of the original planting, the weeds having completely taken over. To my astonishment, she gave me a lesson in ericaceous plants, uncovering one small but still well-formed specimen. Contrary to her earlier claims, she knew plenty about gardening, the Latin names of nearly every plant in the garden being just the tip of her knowledge.

'...An offspring from one of the first few plants to come to the United States. Charles propagated it himself; *Rhododendron yakushimanum*,' she explained, deftly using a spade to cut away the encroaching weeds.

Yakushimanum. The word kept cropping up, only this time I had found its origins, realising that this was not only what he was trying to say in the hospital, but probably the very plant he was referring to. I enjoyed watching Marion clear the ground. She worked effectively, with little wasted effort, all the while explaining numerous properties of the plant – that it originated from the Japanese island of Yakushima, and how its blossom was in perfect proportion to the delicate leaves that surrounded it.

Marion offered more advice than I was used to hearing but she was in good spirits and together we went on to weed the whole bed. As we worked on, I couldn't resist bringing up the diaries, specifically Charles's separation from his brother during the D-Day landings, something which I could not get out of my mind.

'It has always been my understanding that most of Jean's platoon never made it to dry land,' she confirmed, her voice suddenly in a quiver. 'Charles never got over that one. He felt that he was responsible for it, that he should have somehow looked after him.'

I remember vividly how her words echoed my similar feelings towards my father, and as I offered the opinion that this was a totally unreasonable notion on the part of Charles, I was at the same time asking myself how a thirteen-year-old boy could have possibly been of any help to a storm-doomed fishing fleet. But this clear, simple argument could not placate such a clinging habit – this particular piece of guilt seeming as solid as the rocks themselves. Marion looked up at me as I wrestled with the notion, and I swear she saw into my burden.

'Towards the end of the war, Charles even stopped off in Normandy, in the pathetic ludicrous hope that Jean might still be alive,' she went on to explain. 'He even traipsed around the beaches, towns and hospitals, if you please!'

As she worked on, I turned to the subject of Dachau and

the musical notation. Her tone darkened even more, like I was pushing into a no-go area, especially when I implied that she must have known something about it.

'Oh yes!' she admitted, her indignation sparking into life. 'I know something about it, all right. It plagued him! And then us!' she snapped, tearing out a weed by its roots and throwing it at my feet. 'When we were first married, while we were creating this garden, the whole war nightmare didn't figure in our lives. But not long after that, he turned to it. As if he could bring back his brother! And the more he tried to work it through, the more unbearable it became!' Her venom raised my pulse, but I kept prying, blatantly asking if he had ever finished it. 'Finished it!' she spat out in punishment for even asking. 'It seems you should have asked him! And why do you think I should have cared?' And as I stared into the bitter face, the notion which had already occurred to me suddenly seemed more than possible: that in her hatred for what the man had put her through, she had destroyed the music. At this we both turned our eyes downward and went back to our weeding, and it must have been a quarter of an hour before she broke the silence.

'I suppose I had my own problems,' she uttered, eyes downturned.

'Your child?' I questioned, and what followed was as if I had opened a door of no return, the look on her face revealing a mind that had done its best to erase the subject, having successfully sat upon the task for the best part of a decade. But with what seemed inevitable, her ancient resentment boiled over once more.

'Oh, he mentions that, does he?'

'Yes. You coming out of the hospital... with bruises.'

'Bruises! And what about a fractured pelvis? And the child!' And when I asked what had happened, she again turned her gaze to the ground. 'I certainly don't recall him taking much notice at the time! Obsessed with that damn monster of a piece! Egocentric bastard... What happened? You want to know what happened? I stormed out one night, sick and tired of his morose behaviour... I'd had a few drinks, a few too many, and lost control of the car... hit a tree. The damned car was brand new.'

The same car, I remember thinking to myself – the old Ford with its damaged front wing, still with a coat of primer red.

By then Marion would not look in my direction, no doubt blaming me for unearthing this particular nightmare, and my suspicions that she had destroyed the music had suddenly grown stronger. And as I was contemplating such a scenario, she suddenly hurled the spade into the ground and stormed off in an uncontrollable rage, very nearly cutting the rhododendron in two.

I came across her sometime later in the summerhouse, a place that up until then she had purposefully stayed away from. She was milling amongst the books, almost as if nothing untoward had happened.

'My God, it is dusty in here,' she offered, running her finger on the edge of the desk and then along one of the bookshelves, as if she enjoyed pushing the dust under her nail. 'I had forgotten he had so many books! And recordings! I remember this, Rachmaninov playing Chopin.'

'Rachmaninov,' I remember repeating in an attempt to correct my previous pronunciation blunder.

'Father drove me all the way to Knoxville to hear him

play. I was barely five years old. As it turned out, it was his last performance.'

'Oh?'

'Yes. He took ill and died some months afterwards,' she recalled before trying out the record player, but with no effect.

I asked her about Charles's playing, half expecting another venomous swing into darkness, but to my surprise her manner softened, almost to tenderness.

'When he was on form it was like nothing else… he could stop people in their tracks. Make me feel… glad to be alive. That all was… sacred.'

That last word left us to browse through the books in silence, and yet I could sense she was still thinking about her husband and some while later she continued.

'He would go through long stretches when he couldn't or wouldn't play. Concerts would be booked but he would cancel at the last moment. Eventually word got around that he couldn't be relied upon. But when it all came together, everything was there. I remember one time the audience wouldn't leave. Oh yes, he could make angels and demons dance to the same tune.'

From that moment, I knew what I dimly believed but had begun to doubt: that behind her wall of resentment and leaking bitterness, she still cared for the man.

'Did you ever perform together?'

'No, not in concert,' she admitted with regret. 'But in between lessons, we did play together. Sometimes for hours. I recall on one particularly warm summer evening, we worked through much of the repertoire for four hands… swapped parts and did it all again. Right through until daybreak,' she extolled, forgetting herself in the fond recollection.

As she continued to browse, I slouched into the one comfortable armchair in the room. 'If you are looking for that damned monster of a piece, I shouldn't waste your time. I've looked everywhere,' I playfully derided, in truth fishing for a clue as to what she might have done with the manuscript.

'New Orleans,' she uttered, peering at the name on a large globe which was perched on a pile of books, and for a moment I vainly hoped her utterance was an admission to its location. 'I took some lovers in that town... or they took me.'

For some reason her splintered reminiscence had removed any desire for the music, suddenly believing that either he had never finished it or had destroyed it himself. *And is it really that important?* I asked myself as Marion kept spinning the globe.

'We bought this from an old junk store, somewhere in the Bible Belt. It had these two holes in it even then: one in Russia and one in the States... Texas to Vermont gone. And this crack around the equator looks to have become worse,' she observed, spinning it a little faster. 'I offered to have it repaired, but Charles preferred it that way. The old storekeeper belonged to some kind of religious sect. Kept going on about how unique it was, that the holes were an omen for the end of the world... a nuclear holocaust. But he sold it. Cash only, if my memory serves me.'

'So, you had some good times?' I ventured, to which her manner suddenly turned wary. 'Charles must have spent a good deal of time down here,' I went on, yet this awkward bit of steering only re-stoked her inner resentment, and even in the fading light I could see her lips tightening white. And all the while the creaking globe spun faster, as if she was Zeus on a bad day, intent on making the winds twist and the tides slosh about.

'The summer before he took the teaching post in Saint Louis, he practically lived down here,' she said eventually, the calm answer, a mere veneer over the twisted emotions within.

'Why didn't you go with him?' I went on, part of me wanting to stoke her fire. And again her silence took hold, as if she did not know where to begin or she had not the words to describe her emotions. I watched her feelings rise and fall.

'It just turned out that way,' came the delayed reply, her eyes ablaze, her fingers gripping the holes in the globe and spinning it ever onwards.

'Hardly an explanation,' was my next jab.

'Well that's all you are going to get!' she thrust back, staring hatefully as the globe juddered at the speed. 'Sick of each other... temporary became permanent.' And at this, Marion wrenched her hand with such a force that the globe twisted off the books, falling and cracking against the floor. The violence brought me to my feet, while she seemed quite happy to see the world break apart at the seams.

'I'm sorry, I'm sorry,' I kept repeating for some reason.

'The thing was already cracked,' she offered as I grappled with the mess.

'But what the hell is this?' I noticed as together we tried to set it up on its stand, chipped and bent as it now was, for the thin opening around the equator was by this time a gaping slit and sticking out of it was what appeared to be a file of papers. We both stared at the odd sight before Marion carefully eased them out and to our amazement, the leaves of paper were covered with musical script.

'Take it outside, so we can see it more clearly,' I suggested, yet even in the dim light, I recognised the bass line from the war diary. We stepped out into the sunshine, but she immediately felt queasy, so I eased her onto a garden bench and sitting down beside her, we sifted the papers in silence.

So suddenly here it was, the laboured answer to all his grief, the source of their trouble and my reason for coming here.

Not long afterwards I followed her up to the house where she tentatively sat down at the piano and one by one, turned through the pages of our new find.

'Rallentando smorzando… just like in the diary I showed you! Well, what do you think?' I pestered, hovering over her shoulder.

'Give me a moment, would you!' she snapped.

'Maybe you would like a drink or something?'

'There is not a drink on earth that could help me now.'

Marion looked it over in silence for what seemed like the longest time, turning the pages, forwards, backwards and forwards again.

'Is it finished?' I had to know.

'Yes, the movement is complete. But if Charles had meant this to be part of a sonata, he would be most unlikely to begin it with something like this. Not one so… so damned grave,' she finally reasoned. 'I am not convinced we have the whole of it.'

And as she continued to study it, her face began to betray an inner dread. For as I was reading the music, albeit with some knowledge of how it came to be, she was doing something more, as if each passage represented some painful moment from her past. Yet she kept turning the pages.

'On second thoughts, I'll take that drink. A bourbon. Make it a large one.'

By then, what remained of any excitement was all but buried.

PEPS

Not long after discovering the second movement, Marion's moods began a swing of extremes, from deep sorrow to a kind of manic cheerfulness. One evening, it must have been a week or so later, we ended our dinner with a delicious butterscotch soufflé.

'One of my specialties!' she exclaimed, telling me to eat it quickly before it drops.

But an hour later she looked resentful and hunted, lingering in the parlour, actively avoiding the new movement before dragging herself off to bed.

As for me, I was torn between following Marion to her bed and keeping my distance. In the end, keeping away won out and I went up to my own room and turned to the diaries. When she'd first mentioned the possibility of another movement, I'd done my best to dismiss it, but gradually her reasoning took hold. The problem was, I had by then scoured both the mansion and the summerhouse and there was not a trace of it to be found. At such times of frustration, I found myself talking to Charles, like he was some sort of lingering spirit looking over my shoulder.

In reading the diaries, it had become my habit to start with the will. I don't know why, since I knew what little it said by heart. Perhaps it was just to remind me of our time together and I liked to look at his simple drawing of a tree, which, as it turned out, would eventually become one of the few clues in my continuing search. But on that hot sticky night, with little hope in my heart, I turned to the earliest diary, for up until then I had only glanced at it briefly, mostly because the impetuous jottings of the eighteen-year-old were next to impossible to read.

He had recently left home for music college and the first few pages were that of a depressed young man, uncomfortable in his own skin. There were repeated jottings about missing his younger brother Jean, along with being unsatisfied with his own playing, and some unflattering remarks on the apparent complacency of his teachers. But then, just as I was about to close its cover and try and get some sleep, an indication of something curious caught my eye, just prior to a group of pages that were stuck together. And after I'd carefully teased them apart, I could hardly believe my eyes!

May 31, 1941 – It keeps throwing itself onto the page. Like I'm just along for the ride! A sonata for piano. A toccata.

June 2 – I showed the idea to old Prof. Wyneman and to my astonishment he didn't dismiss it!

June 12 – Peps. Last week, unprovoked, Wyneman stopped me in the hallway and asked how it was going.

And he meant it. It is late now but tomorrow I will finish it.

Those three short entries raised my blood, and there was that word again, *Peps.* A place... some part of the college, or a bar perhaps? I remember going straight off to tell Marion the news, but she had already left for Atlanta.

To keep myself from dwelling on the matter, I went to work on one of the lower lawns, my mind still in a whirl, all the time wondering what I could possibly do with this new information. After about an hour of pulling weeds, I became fed up and went into town to Dawson's Hardware to purchase a can of weedkiller, a concoction that the salesman assured me would kill everything but the grass. But on one particularly hot afternoon, a few days after spreading the treatment, to my shock and disbelief the lawn looked to be beginning to turn a little yellow.

At first, I tried to convince myself that it was merely a play of light, but as the days passed the yellow grew stronger and eventually everything curled up and died! I must have messed up the dose, the proportions of water and poison. In any event, I remember feeling so bloody angry as I dragged a load of weeds and bramble down to the bottom terrace to add to a pile of rubbish, which had built up over the previous few months. By then, the mound contained a multitude of things: old newspapers, cardboard boxes, mouldy bits of carpet, roots, branches, uprooted diseased shrubs, leaves and grass clippings. For whatever reason I had let it grow into a mountain, towering up over my head, almost to where the columns met the cupola of the little temple.

Well, that afternoon, in a kind of fever pitch, I sloshed

a whole can of petrol over the pile, dripped a path up the steps to the next terrace and lit the gaseous fuse. The little blue flames sizzled away at a ravenous speed, meeting the mountain of rubbish with a low boom and a shock wave that rocked me, and in a matter of seconds the pyre was a crackling roar, the heat so fierce that I was soon forced up onto the next terrace. I remember the orange flames leaping up out of the thick swirling smoke, all set against the white temple, the cottonwoods and the darkening sky.

I hardly dare admit this, even now to myself, but as I lay down on the dying grass, watching the red-hot cinders float up and away, there was a moment when I might have turned the whole damned can of poison on the rest of the garden. Where these feelings of wanton destruction rose from, I wouldn't like to say. Maybe I just didn't want to tolerate such absolute stupidity; or is it that this destruction is present more often than I care to admit – dormant but there? A kind of wanton slide into meaningless degradation. I do know that there are times when care comes as a burden too heavy and my mind persuades itself into a darkness, an abyss which it unreasonably seems to crave. Not a pretty sight, if you look too closely... as I think someone said somewhere.

And as I lay there, feeling the heat and steam, listening to the sounds of matter popping and sizzling into flame, my thoughts strayed to the first time I had laid eyes on the unkempt, uncared-for place. From the very beginning I had been intrigued by what sort of person inhabited it, and after meeting her I gradually came to realise that it was no longer just the music that gave meaning to the journey. And yet, it's not that I had any great desire to change the ways of another, my nature tending to let people go their own way. But given that this strange circumstance had brought us together, something made me want to understand what sort of stuff she was made of. And I suppose, by inference... myself.

Despite such inner darkness, I did not do anything so rash as to level the garden with a can of weed killer, but instead, fell fast asleep in the sick yellow grass while the pyre raged hotter and higher. It was a calm warm night and when some hours later I half heard a low boom, which in my dream-like state I mistook for one of those Atlantic groaners, an odd sensation passed over me, like being in a snowstorm, only the flakes were warm. Something must have exploded within the pile, and when I awoke in the early hours of the next morning, it was to the sight of grey-white cinders floating down out of a ghostly light. My mind had no answer. Strange was hardly the word, for in the heat of that afternoon I had stripped naked, and along with most of the garden I was being covered in the weightless ash.

Feeling exhausted by all the inner turmoil, I fell back asleep, and waking later that same morning it was as if I had been transported back in time to Pompeii in 79AD, the sole survivor from Mount Vesuvius's suffocating blanket of waste. Or more frightening still, that one of the ancient gods had granted my diabolical wish to destroy the terraces. But I had to laugh as I ascended the steps through the unreal vision, for along with the poison, I had purchased some special ash that was to give nutrients to the roses. And there the box was, still sitting unopened amongst the plants, their delicate pink petals now completely covered in the stuff.

THE GREENSKEEPER

The next day, a long hard rain washed the ash into the ground and after about a week the patch of lawn was looking like a giant slice of brown bread.

Marion and I were working in the garden, she preparing a flowerbed for some new ericaceous shrubs and I, lower down, circling around the inert flat corpse. I remember feeling foul and trapped, and as I wiped the sweat from my brow, I looked up towards the house to see a white-haired man handing a few healthy-looking plants to Marion. They chatted for a while and just when I was about to go to the stream and try and forget about gardening, he started down the steps towards me, presumably to have a closer look at my carbuncle. He never said much, he didn't have to, for by the way he examined the plants and looked over the terraces, anyone with half an eye could tell he knew about gardens; with me, standing there, feeling like a third-rate clown in a circus ring.

'No matter how long you look at it, it ain't gonna turn green, son,' he opened with a glint in his eye.

'Oh, it might come back,' I argued stubbornly.

'Yea, sometime in late August… if it rains every morning and shines every afternoon. And when it does, most of it will be couch grass and dandelions.'

'It is my problem!' I croaked back foolishly.

'Then I'll be sure to put in a prayer for you,' he offered simply before turning back up the steps and saying his goodbyes to Marion.

A little while later, I came up to where she was working, my mood if anything even worse than before.

'That old guy seems to think he knows something.'

'Certainly, many believe he does,' she offered confidently, handing me a spade and a potted *Pieris*.

'Who is he anyway?'

'He was the gentleman who prevented you from choking to death on your tongue.' Her words sucking my throat dry as my blind pride turned to humiliation. 'It's not quite deep enough,' she rightly noticed as I wilfully tried to push the plant into the meanly cut hole. 'His name is Zeke, Zeke Dodd.' In hearing this, my jaw must have hit the ground and for a split second I didn't know why. Once again, Charles's sleep-talk came flooding back.

'He said this in a dream!'

'In a dream? Who said what in a dream?'

'Charles. At the time… I thought it was just the sleepy ramblings of a madman. He… he came out with the name of *Zeke*! Amongst other things.'

'Zeke was a good friend of the Peccatte family. On occasion he would spend the weekend here and help us with the garden,' she explained, handing me another potted plant – a withered-looking specimen which was propped up with a bamboo stake.

'Where did you get this?' I remember asking, thinking that she had been diddled.

'Oh, the nursery man threw it in.'

'Threw it out is more like it!'

'Sometimes the runts turn out the best,' she insisted. 'Put it over here.'

'But that's where it was!'

'Then I do believe I was right the first time! Now start digging, would you!'

'So, who is Zeke? Some sort of garden expert?' I had to know, this time making the hole good and ample.

'You could say that... Now lots of water,' she ordered, holding up the watering can. 'He is the head-keeper at The Aglaia National.'

'The Aglaia National? Some sort of racecourse, is it?'

'No, dear, a golf club... or more accurately, *the* golf club.'

This, along with the bamboo stake, reminded me of the old, broken golf iron which held up the tomato plant back in the Chicago apartment.

'Hector, Charles's father, had a plant nursery next to the distinguished establishment,' she explained while handing me another pot. 'Not too deep now.'

'Am I right in saying that this Aglaia Club bought Charles's father out, towards the end of the war?' I asked, by now recalling something about it in one of the diaries.

'Yes... Charles always reckoned it was only a matter of time. Hector specialised in ericaceous plants. A well respected expert on the subject... which explains his special affections for this area of the garden. Not quite deep enough,' she complained.

I shook my head in disbelief, having shown her the depth

at least twice. But strangely, her orders soothed some part of me, so I took out a few more spadefuls.

'Much better. I'll make a gardener out of you yet.'

We worked on through the morning, putting in two more rhododendrons, three azaleas and another *Pieris japonica*.

'So, maybe it would be worth talking to Zeke?' I proposed as the last plant went in.

'Do you honestly believe that will help to find the rest of the music? Assuming that it exists at all,' she offered doubtfully.

'You said yourself that the sonata is incomplete as it stands.'

'Incomplete! Charles was quite capable of that!' she cried, heeling in the new plant as if suddenly trying to bury it. 'More water, lots more water!'

'But you've seen the references in that early diary. When he was at music college, he was passionate about composing something! Well, Zeke knew him then... so maybe, just maybe, he could shed some light on the matter.'

She poured the water around the new specimen, trying to repair some of her heavy footwork. And when I tried to help, she would have none of it.

'Are all the Irish like you?' she accused.

'Like what?'

'Dreamers chasing dreams... and a dead man's dreams, at that!'

'What about Peps?' I then had to ask. 'Straight to Peps.'

'Peps? It means nothing to me. Why do you ask?'

'Something else Charles said in one of his dreams.'

Marion just shook her head in disbelief and walked up to the house.

THE AGLAIA NATIONAL

I had to put the phone in Marion's hand and plead, yet when she actually made the call, she was as charming as pie – a phrase of Mrs. Drake's, someone I would still visit when I was tired of my own cooking. And Marion's call paid off, it being arranged that I was to meet Zeke Dodd at the famous Aglaia National, and afterwards I remember asking her what made the club so special.

'Some would maintain it is the closest thing this grand nation has got to holy ground! And I dare say, there are men who have gladly handed over their souls for a membership card,' was the way I think she put it.

On the morning of the appointment, she handed me a packed lunch and the keys to the old Ford, and I tried to persuade her to come along, but she would have none of it.

'No, I think not. That sort of wealth gives me the creeps.' And when I asked if she found the idea of living in mansions too much to take, her eyes rolled up in irritation. 'Believe me, you have never laid eyes on that sort of money! This here place would be no more than a summer cottage to the men who have made that establishment!'

In all my trepidation and excitement, I don't remember much about the trip, other than the fact that the various neighbourhoods I drove through encompassed a wide spectrum of the haves and have-nots, and that the stars and stripes were more abundant with the former, fluttering above the flat, well-watered lawns.

A big fat guard put out his hand and brought me to a stop at the auspicious entrance, looking me over like I was the plague on wheels. And only after carefully writing down my business and making a telephone call, did he press the button to open the silently moving gates. My first sight was a huge wave of brightly coloured azaleas, the view shockingly contrasted by the fact that moments before I had witnessed some young black kid – he couldn't have been more than ten – running around in rags, without shoes. And another, a little older, who could have been his brother, pushing drugs. And my mind couldn't quite equate that this grey hopeless scene seemed not much more than a stone's throw from those pearly gates.

I pulled into an almost empty car park and as I stepped from the old Ford to take in the heavenly sight, Marion's remark about *holy ground* echoed in my mind. For as I was to learn, this was not so much a place of sport as the ultimate shrine to an exclusive way of life – one of the more untouchable American dreams.

What limousines there were told the story, especially when set against Marion's rusty heap. Stretching my stiff limbs, I gazed over what looked to be the grounds of a national treasure but in a way felt more like some strange sort of security establishment. There was not a person in sight, but I certainly felt like I was being watched.

As a young boy I remember the first time I ever laid eyes on a golf course. There were sheep rambling about on it and one of the fleecy creatures was intent on holding his ground in front of a man franticly swinging a club in the long grass. For the longest time I actually believed sheep were part of the game. What I did imagine on a course like this was a few company executives intent on their pastime, but there were none. In fact, I must have been there for nearly half an hour before laying eyes on a living soul and he was a gardener, clipping a hedge that already looked to be perfection in the art of topiary. I couldn't resist bending down to touch the green carpet, just to confirm that it was real! For this was not like any lawn I had ever seen, with no sign of any moss, or a weed, or even where a weed used to live, just uniform blades, reflecting and absorbing the light in perfect regimentation. And another thing that struck me was the quietness of it all, for our garden was tranquil but here even the birds seemed well-behaved.

With a growing discomfort I made my way to the clubhouse, its classical pillars dazzling white in the bright sunshine. And just as I was having second thoughts about being there at all, the head butler greeted me at the front entrance.

'Good morning, sir. You are here to meet with Mr. Dodd,' speaking in that tranquil southern drawl, an accent which by now I had grown used to.

My face must have given away my surprise at what I had seen so far, for he then asked if anything was the matter.

'I guess I just expected there to be more people about,' I replied.

'This is a winter club, sir, the summers being uncomfortably hot and humid,' came the polite explanation, as he ushered me into a reception lounge.

The walls of the room were covered with photographs of famous men in the golfing world, along with heads of state and past presidents. Not club presidents but United States Presidents – a Mr. Dwight D. Eisenhower taking pride of place. After a good ten minutes of complete silence, the kind of silence I liken to an empty church, the butler returned and sent me down to what he referred to as the practice green, where Mr. Dodd would meet me.

From this meeting point, as I gazed out at the fantastic, sculptured playground, it began to sink in that this man, who I probably owed my life to and who I later insulted with my blatant ignorance, was actually in charge, that in a very real sense this was his garden.

It wasn't long before a golf cart appeared in the distance on one of the magnificent rolling fairways. It came to a smooth stop some yards away and like everything else, hardly made a sound. With a relaxed smile, Zeke Dodd stepped out. He was shorter than I remembered, perhaps because of his higher position that day in the garden, probably over seventy, but spry on his feet. A shaggy silver moustache matched his head of hair, setting off his tanned, animated features. Unlike before, I liked his face, it being clear and open, with a touch of playfulness behind the eyes. And as I was to learn, he was a man of depth, yet I sensed somehow not altogether comfortable with his world. No doubt he realised my awkwardness, as without a word he motioned towards the splendid, manicured turf under our feet.

'If I recall, brown is more your colour,' he ventured as an opening gambit.

'Yes, but I could be persuaded.'

At this he offered his hand and without another word, ushered me into the cart. We were soon rolling over the fairways.

'I never had the chance to thank you for what you have done for me,' I began to apologise. 'You must have had a shock that day.'

Zeke Dodd nodded his head and went on to explain how when he pulled up to the mansion and noticed the paper boy staring down at something moving on the grass, he assumed it was an injured dog. But when he came closer, there I was in full fit, flailing and frothing.

'When you started to choke, I just laid you on your side to free your tongue and ordered the boy to run off and get help.'

While listening to his explanations, it began to dawn on me that the one who phoned the hospital had not been Marion at all, but him, and as we continued through the mysterious setting, I tried to explain that despite appearances there had been more successes than failures in Marion's garden.

'Listen, young man, over the years I have watched in despair as that garden fell into ruin. There were occasions when I even considered trying to bring it back, but as you might imagine, this place demands everything I've got, and then some. So it has boiled down to cutting the front lawn and taking Marion out for a meal once in a while. And as I'm sure you have discovered, she is not the most social of animals… Believe me, my heart was lifted when I set eyes on your efforts.'

We soon came to a stop beside a large putting green. Zeke got out of the cart and squatted down beside it.

'I think you would appreciate that on such a surface as this, any flaw, however insignificant, will instantly show itself. In my early days here, I mowed it with a machine that had an oil leak. A slow but constant drip. In those days we serviced our own machines and were responsible for their upkeep. So, there was no excuse,' he calmly explained, scanning the green's every undulation. 'Do you know what mineral oil does to a plant? A few days later there were little brown drip lines running up and down, over the whole surface. After one hell of a dressing down, the head man sent me out here to tend to every one of those lines. I must have been on it for two weeks solid. And all the time my job was in the balance.' He stood up and looked me directly in the eye. 'So you have not cornered the market in foolish mistakes.'

After that, he invited me to "explain this sonata business". I told him about our recent find in the summerhouse and how there seemed a good chance there was another movement to come. I tried to fill him in on my own experiences with Charles and I could tell he had a soft spot for the man.

'It was Charles's diaries and to some extent his dream that—'

'Dream?'

'Yes. In the hospital. He mentioned your name. Called it out: *Zeke! On fifteen!*'

'On fifteen?' he repeated.

Without another word, Zeke motioned for me to get back into the cart.

'And Jean, he mentioned his brother Jean. And also Peps, *straight to Peps*,' I continued to explain as we whooshed along.

Zeke Dodd looked at me with a knowing glint in his eye. 'Fifteen refers to the hole. And as for Peps, it is not only a man, it's a house. Or to be more accurate, *was* a house.'

When I heard this, I pulled out one of the photographs from the Chicago apartment, the one of the somewhat ramshackle wooden dwelling surrounded by shrubbery, and he needed but a mere glance before nodding in confirmation.

'That's the name the boys gave it. As you may know, Hector Peccatte was of French extraction. Grew up in Louisiana. He kept to his mother tongue when describing his profession. *Pépiniériste*. Charley and Jean just shortened it to Peps.'

We continued through the strangely beautiful landscape and eventually Zeke pointed towards a large, ancient-looking magnolia in the distance.

'We are approaching the old nursery boundary. The actual house used to stand in that clearing. Just behind the fifteenth green.'

We pulled up close and got out of the cart, and as he slowly looked around, it became apparent that the area meant a great deal to him, his eyes betraying ghosts that still lingered. I had the feeling that it was not his custom to talk so candidly, especially to a relative stranger, yet for some reason it was time for his tongue to loosen.

'The club had ambitions for more land and the plant nursery had always been on their agenda. At first, they made Hector an offer, no more than what it was worth, and when he refused and refused again on a higher price, they brought in some smart lawyer, even offered him a membership if he could come up with something. This lawyer did what he had been trained to do and made a case for a boundary dispute.'

'So Hector had to sell.'

'Not right off. They only managed a few thin acres but upped their offer once more. When that failed, they laid low for a year or so before coming up with yet another price. This time it was huge; if I recall, over ten times what the place was worth. Yet still old Hector wouldn't budge. I mean, it was his place! His life! And not a bad life, at that!'

It didn't take much to see that Zeke had never liked the way the club had handled the matter and, looking deeper, that he in some way had been a part of it and felt ashamed for what they had done to the Peccatte family.

'As I recall, it was finally purchased in May of forty-three. No, forty-four,' he corrected himself. 'But work didn't start till the summer. June fourth, to be precise. It was my birthday, so I could hardly forget.'

'That's coming up soon.'

'Yep… seventy-five. My official retirement. There have been times when I've almost called it quits, but one thing or another has kept me put,' he admitted, guiding me closer to the tall magnolia. 'The old wooden sign used to hang about here. *Pépinière Peccatte* written in big black letters. That was the rough part, for by the end, Hector's health was suffering badly and with no wife and his two sons at war, the place was falling apart.'

'And what happened to his wife?'

'I only ever recall meeting her once, not long after I had first come to work here. She was a Yankee from somewhere up north… Wisconsin, I believe. Hector would hardly talk of her, other than to say how much she loved her boys and how all their musicality had come from her. But the story I heard is that she was prone to bouts of depression and ended up in some mental hospital up there. And when she found out that Jean was missing in action, she wandered off one cold winter's night and froze to death.'

'So he finally sold up.'

'Yep… with the fate of his boys in the balance and his health failing. The sad thing was he had done next to nothing to prepare for the inevitable, and truth be known, the whole thing turned into one hell of a mess. At the last moment he even changed his mind, told the club that he would give the money back. But it was too late for such nonsense. They had to practically drag him away.'

'You weren't there?'

'Oh yea, I was there, all right. I did nothing one way or the other. The police were brought in to do the dirty work. But I can still see Hector now, through the screen door. Standing in his porch. All alone. Beside himself he was, calling out for his boys. I went to see him a few weeks after it was all over… already rotting away in a brand new old folks home, and a few months later he was a mere shadow of the man I had known.'

I stood silent while Zeke eyed the ground with an uncomfortable concentration, glancing up occasionally as if the house was still in view. Unprovoked, he went on talking, as if he had to get it off his chest.

'At times he may have been an awkward old cuss, but when it came to matters of plant husbandry, he was a fountain of knowledge. I learnt a hell of a lot from him, when most men in his position wouldn't have conceded a damn thing,' he admitted, swinging his arm in a wide circle. 'He knew this land before the course existed. Knew it deeply. Even talked of a sacred Indian burial site. The whole area is still imbued with the man… he lingers… at least in the opinion of this old fool.'

It was about then that I pulled out the will diary and

turned to Charles's last testament. The words had been written in strong black lettering over the now familiar pencil drawing of that tree. I handed it to Zeke and by the look in his eyes it was plain that he now understood something of what had gone on between us.

'The tree?' I suggested, looking up at the magnolia's lush foliage.

'Yes, could be,' he agreed. 'This magnolia has always been a landmark. I promised Hector we would keep it. It's bigger now but still I can't set eyes on it without imagining the house.'

'And where exactly was the house?'

'Many think it stood where the green lies and to this day, some of the older members still refer to it as Pépiniér's Green. But in point of fact, it was situated behind... just there, on the edge of the fairway. Anyway, after persuading the powers that be, we stopped short with the green placement. When the house was levelled, the only thing we added was that bunker... the basement is still down there.'

'Still there?'

'Yep. The equipment moved in right after Hector had left. And the Club Committee pushed us hard to get it done... too hard. It was at a time when they were courting some president elect, so, to save time, the top was just bulldozed flat,' he recalled, pointing to a barely discernible line on the grass. 'I'm surprised the ground hasn't sunk more over the years.'

A few weeks after our meeting, Marion invited Zeke to the mansion for lunch, where he gave me some solid advice on various aspects of the garden, and shortly after that I returned to his domain, armed with a theory to put to him. We met at the maintenance shack where all the machines and equipment were kept, and this time his army of underlings were tending the course from top to bottom. I had never seen so many different kinds of lawn mowers and the like. I also met Zeke's right-hand man, Eugene Sartory, or "E" as Zeke called him, and although he was a man of few words, I got the distinct feeling that nothing much passed him by and he was very good at his job.

The minute I arrived, E handed out some cold sodas from an ancient-looking red cooler machine that stood outside under a lilac bush and beckoned me to take a seat on a sun-bleached railway sleeper. Behind, stood an old mechanical digger, rising out of the waist-high grass like some sort of sleeping prehistoric reptile.

'That is the very machine we used to level the Peccatte house. Still goes, doesn't it, E?' Zeke said. E merely nodded his head and finished his soda in one gulp.

To their curiosity, I then revealed the two movements of Charles's sonata, Zeke carefully lifting the music out of my hands and leafing through its pages.

'Mr. Zeke, I never knew you could read music?' E queried.

'Oh, I play the piano some. Do battle with a few of the classics. But mostly it's merely ragtime tunes,' Zeke admitted with increasing interest in what lay before him.

I followed with the early diary. 'Here he speaks of working on what I believe to be the first movement... in his student days.' E quickly looked it over before handing it on to his boss. 'It is one of many diaries which I found in the summerhouse.'

The old man eagerly took the little book from E's hands while I pointed to the reference to Peps, the family house where he was living at the time.

'Yes, that's before the war,' he confirmed.

'Do you remember him doing any composing?'

'He certainly used to play the piano a great deal. And not just solo. He and Jean played together. Violin sonatas.'

'They were close?'

'Oh yeah. Charles had infinite patience with Jean when it came to accompanying him. And it paid off. I remember they gave a few concerts in the church. They were good.'

The sun was getting hot, and Zeke brought out his handkerchief to wipe his brow while he considered my earlier question.

'I remember Hector complaining about Charles on more than one occasion. At times they could get into the most god-awful rows, mostly about Charles not pulling his weight as regards to the plant work... I remember one day, him moaning that when the boy got in one of his "inspirational states", as he used to call it, he was useless for anything. Hector claimed he would lock himself in his bedroom and not come out for hours on end.'

I pointed to the phrase in the diary. '*A sonata for piano. A toccata!* As you can see, he was definitely in one of those states this time.'

Zeke nodded in contemplation and as he leafed through the rest of the diary, his interest continued to grow. My thoughts returned to the fifteenth hole and that little sunken ditch that marked where the house used to stand.

'Would you happen to know where Charles's bedroom was?'

'Ah...' he hesitated, looking up from the diary. 'Downstairs, I believe.'

'On the ground floor, or in the basement?' I pressed.

'The basement... yes, in the basement. As I recall, Charley always suffered from the heat, and it was cooler down there.'

'So, in effect, it is still there.'

With a wry smile, E relieved me of my empty soda bottle and turned to his boss. 'Would I be right in thinking that this man has an inclination to dig up the fifteenth fairway of Aglaia National?'

And to my surprise, Zeke looked at me in a way which suggested that what I was implying was not completely out of court, that at least part of him was prepared to speculate on the prospects of such an outrageous notion.

'But what could possibly be left down there after near on thirty-five years?' E rightly asked.

'True enough, it has been a long while,' Zeke admitted. 'But on the other hand, E, as you well know, that spot is on high ground and once you get a few feet down, it's mostly sand. And not much rots in sand.'

'Let's say there *is* something down there. What sort of chance do you have of getting such a motion past Mr. Barnes and his stony-faced committee?' E questioned while Zeke returned to the book. 'And if you don't mind me asking, what makes you so keen?' E continued to press.

'Who said I'm keen? Let's just say, that old place was special. I can still remember Charles's playing drifting across the fairways… on into the evening. That's when I first heard a Chopin nocturne.'

E's smile returned, repeating, 'Chopin nocturne,' as if he just wanted to say something that had never passed his lips before. 'Never knew you were such an old romantic.'

'Old romantic!' Zeke scowled in mock anger. 'Getting back to practicalities, I suggest you stretch those legs and get out and cut number nine fairway before dark!'

Looking back on it, I suspect that Zeke's interest in my

idea was a mixture of emotion. For not only did he have a great affinity with the Peccattes and all that surrounded the place, he had never really come to terms with the way the Club Committee had pressured the old man to sell, and who knows, there may well have been other dark corners between him and the men who made the rules. Perhaps, too, he felt at his age there was nothing much to lose and something inside him wanted to go out with a bang. For whatever reason, by the time we had driven back to the car park, his mind was already working over the best way to approach the matter.

'I will talk to Ned Barnes. God knows he gives the word *autocrat* a new meaning, so don't get your hopes up... but he owes me a few favours,' he reasoned, his attention turning towards the old Ford. 'I had one just like that until the Club presented me with that one over there,' he said, pointing to a shiny new Lincoln Continental. 'Fifty years' service... yep, just like that,' he repeated, running his hand over the primer painted front wing.

And I could see his mind clicking back in time, perhaps to Marion's accident, before returning to the venture at hand, assuring me that as soon as he had a chance to talk with the Club President, he would let me know.

THE MEETING

True to his word, about a week later Zeke telephoned to say that a meeting had been arranged with the Club Committee and that I was to come looking my best and ready to do battle. By then Charles's tweed was looking kind of scruffy, but given its history it seemed only right that I should wear it on such an occasion. Without asking, Marion took the jacket away and had it cleaned and its elbows darned. The brogues were also past their best, but after a good session of spit and polish they were looking pretty good.

'You are almost presentable,' she had to admit as I finished combing my hair on the appointed day.

'Marion… would you come to the meeting with me?'

'No… I don't think so,' she answered with a quiver in her voice.

From the moment Zeke had arranged the meeting, I wanted her to come, but for some reason my feelings only came out at the last moment.

'Look, I woke up last night in a cold sweat! Convinced that the whole thing was mad! And this morning, I was about ready to call it off… I would very much like you to be there,' I pleaded.

She turned away and said nothing for a time and I was surprised when she changed her mind. Yet as soon as she had relented, a look of worried confusion enveloped her face.

'What's the matter?'

'Oh nothing… I was just wondering what I should wear.'

'What you should wear?' And with hardly a thought, I blurted out, 'Something that… that shows your spirit.'

'Shows my spirit?' she mocked, always uncomfortable with such notions.

'And your legs.'

That sent her packing. She went to the back of her wardrobe and found the same indigo coloured dress that she had been wearing in the photograph of her at the piano, and as we got out of the car, I remember wondering how this could possibly be the same person who first greeted me at the door of the mansion. Then, she had looked ten years older than her forty-three years; now, as I watched her walk towards the clubhouse in the dappled sunlight, she looked ten younger.

The place had a different feel about it this time, mostly due to the number of people about. As for the obvious wealth, she was right of course. You could smell it if you had a cold. Not that it was being flaunted, other than in the size and quality of the cars. No, these men prided themselves on their conservative outlook, their disciplined code of conduct, as if there was only one way to approach life – that is, if you had the vault to back it up.

On that warm summer day, I felt proud to be walking beside Marion and as we were introduced to various committee members, she showed great charm. As for Zeke, when he set eyes on her, he nearly fell over.

'Who is this?' he asked me with such sincerity as to be believed. 'I'm very glad to make your acquaintance, madam,' came his deadpan introduction, but a few moments later he couldn't resist embracing her as if she was his long-lost daughter. 'Sean, I'll be going in shortly to give them my usual report on the course. I expect you'll be up soon after that. I'll introduce you, but then it's your show.'

By the time Zeke was called to the boardroom, my nerves were beginning to show and I went off to get a stiff drink at the bar to try and calm them.

'So what is this Holy Grail rumour about?' I overheard one member saying to another as they propped up the bar.

'Ah, old Zeke Dodd must be losing his marbles, wanting to spend time and money on such nonsense.'

'Isn't he retiring soon?'

'I do believe he has had his day,' the younger one decreed.

I could have done with not hearing such talk and I quickly downed my drink and went back to our table. By then, Marion was feeling fidgety and it seemed an age before one of the butlers approached and politely informed me that it was time.

When I walked into that room of stony-faced men, a strange sensation swept over me, as if suddenly being dropped into a bygone era. Perhaps it was their dress and the strict decorum of it all, as if no one would have batted an eye if Mr. Eisenhower had walked in and announced that war had been declared. Oh, I was politely shown to my seat, but in a way that felt like I was on trial, like some prisoner on death row pleading for clemency. And as I gazed along the dark oak table, I got a strong disagreeable vibe from Ned Barnes, a closed-faced, controlling man on a well-worn road, silently writing notes. And I couldn't help noticing as I walked past him that his small machine-like printing had completely filled the little notepad, as if some sort of crime would be committed if every little space had not been accounted for. I saw a face that was used to getting its own way, and I would have bet my bottom dollar that he had already made up his mind, that underneath he was barely tolerating such a quirky venture and was merely going through the motions in some sort of sham respect for his head greenskeeper.

Zeke gave me a generous introduction and despite my bout of nerves, I began my case well, giving them a history of the venture while trying not to get bogged down in details. By then most of them had perked up, but when I started to emphasise the quality of the music, I got the distinct feeling that they were suddenly hearing gibberish. The most important part, as far as I was concerned, seemed to have no value for them and when I handed round the early diary which showed that Charles was living there at the time he was writing the piece, their faces changed little – as if they were in some sort of high-stake poker game.

'Your story is most interesting, young man, but is it likely that such a piece of music would be written over such a long period of time?' came the expected opening salvo.

I answered with my prepared speech about Beethoven and Wagner and how they had sometimes spent many years on particular compositions. I seem to recall finishing with, 'I don't think it really matters what we call it, nor does it matter that Charles Peccatte had meant them to be one piece. I happen to believe that he did, but the point is that there is evidence another score exists!'

'But the fact remains that it is one hell of a long shot and most unlikely that there will be anything at all left down there. Let alone some sheet of music,' came the next one.

'Judging from Charles's existing efforts, I expect it will be more than just *some* sheet of music,' I firmly corrected the comfortable fat man, his face growing pink at my change of tone. And with this and what was to come, there is little doubt that I pushed their stubborn pride too far when my true feelings bubbled over. 'It is the declaration of a young man struggling to find his voice, which might just be buried down there!' I called out to the collection of self-satisfied judges. 'And although that may seem a trifling matter to such an established group as yourselves, I for one consider it to be of value. If each of you think back through your own lives, perhaps you could remember a time, a particular moment, when something needed to be said... if only to try and clarify... to in some way express what it is to be alive!'

They were no more surprised than I at what had come out of my mouth. And by that time, feeling pretty self-righteous, I opened my valise to show them what we had already found, but to my disbelief when I reached into the leather wallet there was nothing. It was my turn for a red face as I searched again, but Charles's music just wasn't there! I remember looking up at Barnes at the far end of the table, convinced that he had guessed what had happened and was happy to let me squirm.

As my mind played back the morning's events to try and unravel the mystery, I vainly checked a third time. I remembered that Marion had been playing that morning, that she must have taken it out and in all the commotion about her decision to come and what dress to wear, she had left it lying on the piano!

'Seeing is believing,' I had reasoned, for if they could examine Charles's work, it would surely have a positive effect, even to these leather-skinned tycoons! And here I was, at the moment of truth, and I had forgotten the most influential piece of evidence! As my mind raged with panic, another member spoke up from further down the long table.

'Nevertheless, young man, I would be inclined to agree with my colleague. After some thirty-odd years in the earth, there'll be nothing but dust! And Zeke, what about the mess this would undoubtedly cause?'

'Regarding what might be still down there—' Zeke began, realising my difficulty, 'as you may or may not know, it is on high ground and one of the best drained areas on the course. Two feet down and it turns to a kind of sandy peat, which must improve our prospects. As to your question regarding any incurring damage, the committee has my word that three weeks after we have covered in the hole and re-turfed it, the ground will look like it was never disturbed.'

Ned Barnes, who had been silent up until then, turned to Zeke.

'I'm sure you will pardon my manners, Zeke, but I fail to see what is in this for you! I mean, this venture just adds to your already strenuous workload.'

Looking straight at the man, Zeke continued, clearly and eloquently. 'All I can say, Ned, is I know from my own experience that Charles Peccatte was an exceptional pianist, and now this young man has brought it to our attention that he was also a composer. To my mind, if there is the slightest chance that this musical composition is down there, we should make the effort.'

Ned Barnes didn't reply to Zeke and without looking in my direction he assured me that they wouldn't take long in making their decision. I remember rising from my chair with the feeling that there must be something more to say. Yet the only thing that came to mind was that I could bring the music back at a later date. But this I knew would have been a pathetic gesture, only serving to show up my incompetence.

When Marion saw us emerge, she rushed over.

'The music?' I demanded, opening the empty valise. I could see the guilt emerging through her questioning eyes and without answering, she turned to Zeke.

'So, what are our chances?'

'Well, I'd be surprised if there is a musician amongst them! And at the moment, they seem wrapped up with the arrival of some head of state... I need a drink.'

As we sipped our drinks, waiting it out with hardly a word passing between us, Zeke got called away on some other business. I was still angry about the music, but I didn't have the heart to rub it in. Marion turned to me, by now her voice in a flutter.

'I took the music out this morning... to work on it... I'm sorry, Sean. I meant to put it back but when you asked me to come, and I had to go and get dressed.'

I felt like yelling, 'How could you?' And in that moment of blind anger I almost accused her of blatant sabotage. But again I said nothing, the truth being that it was my fault. *Would it really have helped to show them the physical evidence? You bet it would!* I rehashed to myself. I watched as that closed, imprisoned look returned to her eyes – a look I had not seen for some time.

At long last the boardroom door opened up and we turned to see Zeke talking with Ned Barnes. Neither was smiling and Zeke looked to be re-arguing our case. Marion downed her drink in one swallow, stood straight up and started walking in their direction.

'Mr. Barnes! Mr. Barnes! Your committee is wrong!' she insisted.

Ned Barnes turned, surprised to see Marion standing right in front of him, her nostrils flaring. She was a sight to behold.

'Madam, I don't believe I have had the privilege,' he began in an effort to stare her down.

'Ah, excuse me. Ned, this is Marion Landray,' Zeke said, equally surprised.

'Right or wrong, Mrs. Landray, we have our reasons. The vote has been cast. Perhaps at a later date we might revisit the issue,' he half-heartedly offered before trying to turn away.

'But Mr. Barnes, you have not even seen the evidence! The actual score, in Charles's hand. I assure you it is most impressive!' she went on.

'I feel sure it is, madam. But we have covered the issues and made up our minds,' he stated firmly, the woman's blatant passion offending his custom.

Yet as he tried to excuse himself, she kept the pressure on. Even Zeke was becoming uneasy.

'Your committee may have talked about it, but they cannot know, cannot honestly understand what it is about.'

'As I said, Mrs. Landray, we have thoroughly discussed—'

'Thoroughly! They have not even heard it!' she

interrupted; by now her mind ablaze. 'It's... it's like being asked to... to choose a painting without even seeing it!' she argued, pointing up to a portrait of the man in front of her.

In disbelief, Barnes turned away a second time and yet she stayed on his heels and by now others were beginning to take an interest.

'What do you like to do?' she demanded of him. 'You like to play this game of golf, correct?'

'Yes, madam... when I have the time!' he admitted impatiently.

'Well, imagine,' she improvised, her mind grappling for some sort of argument, 'imagine approaching the first green and there was no flag... no hole... there would hardly be much meaning in continuing now, would there?'

Ned Barnes turned to Zeke with an accusing stare which screamed, *look what you have started, you old fool!* Then he turned again to the impassioned woman.

'If there was no hole, madam, Mr. Dodd would certainly have something to answer for!'

I had never seen or heard Marion like this. Her argument may have been bizarre but there was no mistaking the passion behind it. And as she continued on, Barnes kept alternating his gaze between the ceiling and her, obviously incensed with what was coming at him, yet I suspect unable to quite keep his eyes off her extraordinary presence.

'Mr. Barnes, do you have any idea what it takes to write such music? Please, give me a chance. Give Charles Peccatte a chance! Let me show you the meaning!'

And by now the Club President was beside himself, yet as more and more members gathered around, he somehow managed to hold his temper.

'By doing what?' he demanded.

'By playing!'

'What?' he finally had to scream.

'The piano! I assume it is playable?' she asked, pointing towards a shiny black Steinway grand in the corner of the lounge.

'Yes, of course, but—'

'Well then, tell your committee to make themselves comfortable while I state my late husband's case! Who knows, they might even enjoy it!'

'Husband?' was all I heard Barnes say as she grabbed my hand and pulled me off towards the piano.

'What the hell are you doing?' I had to ask as she lifted up the piano lid.

'I know the last movement well enough,' she reasoned.

In the background we could hear Zeke doing his best to organise the concert.

'What nonsense, Zeke! I've got to be in the city by four!' piped up one committee member.

'Come on, now. It will not take long, and we need only our good manners to hear the woman out,' Zeke reasoned firmly.

With a mix of emotions they began to take their seats, except for Barnes, who preferred to stand, crossing his arms with a look of a sea captain in the face of a mutiny.

'Does she have the music?' Zeke came up and whispered to me.

'No,' I admitted with some terror.

Marion waited for quiet, or at least as quiet as it was going to get, for by now word had spread through the clubhouse and other members and even staff were beginning to enter. It wasn't long before the room was all but packed, whereupon Marion stood up from the piano stool, cleared her throat, and spoke aloud.

'For those of you who do not know, we have recently discovered the second and third movements of a piano sonata by Charles Peccatte. I will now play the third, completed shortly before he died.'

As she sat down and collected herself, I remember looking over at Zeke and despite all his embarrassment, it was obvious that he was very proud of Marion. Her start was tentative, and it wasn't long before she had a memory lapse. Her nerves were showing, but she had enough composure to return to the opening, and by then you could have heard a pin drop. She began again, gradually finding her confidence, relaxing into a splendid rendition and the more she played, the better it became, filling the place with a rich, passionate, sonorous sound.

She finished to a complete silence before applause gradually began to rise up, it being blatantly clear that the crowd was deeply moved. As for the committee members who had remained, their feelings were harder to read, and when the clapping died away to raised eyebrows and murmurs of praise, Ned Barnes slipped out of the room, his red face betraying an inner rage.

'I hope it made up for my blunder,' Marion apologised as we walked to the car.

'You more than made up for it. It was fine playing. Very fine! Charles would have been proud. Zeke is going to have another word with Ned Barnes and phone us as soon as he knows anything.'

'Do you think it will be enough to sway them?'

'I wouldn't like to say. One of the committee members came up and shook my hand and would hardly let go. But with most I just couldn't tell. As for Barnes...'

'Barnes has forsaken love,' she said in a way that suggested she knew something about it.

MORE PAIN THAN POETRY

During the drive back, I couldn't get her performance out of my mind. There had been something deeply impressive about it, hard to describe in musical terms alone. Like the music and the player fundamentally needed each other – as if each had been released, lifting each other in turn, up into the land of the living.

That afternoon, back at the mansion, we felt restless waiting for Zeke to phone. I went outside to do some weeding, just to keep myself busy, and when the phone finally rang, Marion took the call in the parlour. I was just below the balcony, and I couldn't hear her exact words but judging by her tone, the news wasn't good. When she came outside, her defeated air said it all.

'But your playing was fine! So very fine!' I protested.

'Quite obviously not fine enough.'

'Oh, you were preaching to the deaf!' I cried in frustration.

'Maybe if I'd played the second movement... not that I can manage the damn thing!' she complained, dragging herself back inside.

Angrily I pulled at a few more weeds, childishly imagining

each to be one of those damned committee members. Accepting that there was no way of consoling her, I wandered down to the summerhouse, and as the reality of the decision sank in, my own despondency began to work me over. I tried to read some book or the other, but words were lost on me, and I soon fell fast asleep. Sometime later I awoke and groggily climbed up the garden steps in the dim evening light.

The parlour reeked of bourbon. Marion was slumped in a chair, the half-empty bottle by her side. The second movement was open on the piano stand and as my footsteps creaked a floorboard, she woke, her eyes looking savagely dark.

'You have been giving this another try?' I said as she tried to pull herself together.

'Yes... I mean, no,' she uttered, downing what was left in her glass and groping for the bottle. I caught it before it toppled onto the floor and put a little more in her glass, but she would not look at me. 'I don't dare... or care... if you would excuse the bad poetry.'

With difficulty she stood up, and when I tried to steady her arm, she would have none of it, taking a few paces towards the offending page of notes.

'His poetry!' she continued contemptuously, throwing back the bourbon and slamming the glass down on the piano. 'More pain than poetry. Tired. So tired. Going to bed.'

She walked out to leave me alone in the darkening room, looking over the music, her words echoing in my mind. It was only eight o'clock, but after such a day I too was not much good for anything. Marion's extreme reaction had, for the moment at least, softened my own disappointment and just to keep my thoughts from spinning round, I cleaned up the house a bit, eventually finding myself on the balcony, watching a bank of large blackening clouds slip along in the evening light. We had been having a run of hot clear days, but change was in the air.

I finally gave in and on the way upstairs, I stopped at Marion's bedroom door; part of me wanted to enter, to try and take her pain away, and mine. There had been moments over the past month when I had wanted to kiss her, and today when she was playing, I had felt glad to know her, but not for the first time I stopped myself and continued up to my bedroom.

Listening to the wind die away, it seemed like a false departure. Suddenly I felt overcome by tiredness, my clothes seeming like heavy shackles which couldn't be got rid of fast enough. Lying there, I wondered about the time between wakefulness and sleep, that moment of being neither here nor there, yet before I knew it, I was there.

It couldn't have been much more than an hour later when a gust of rain-filled wind slammed the bedroom shutter so hard that I sprang out of bed, still half asleep. And as I scrambled to lift the sash, that damned *wave* returned, the conjure so real that I ducked down to let it pass, squatting, legs quivering, my mind confused as to what was inside and what was out. Another loud bang brought me around and I reached out into the torrent of wind and water to pull the shutter in.

This done, the sound of the piano became audible, and I remember thinking it must be close to dawn but when I eventually found my watch it wasn't even midnight. Pulling on my trousers, I tiptoed down the two flights of stairs and as the music grew louder and wilder, I crept silently to the entrance of the parlour, crouched down in the darkness and watched from a distance. The only source of illumination, other than the odd pulse of grey lightning, was a flickering standard lamp. One of the windows was wide open and the sash curtains were thrashing away as if dancing to the notes.

The woman was completely wrapped up with the dreaded second movement, in some wild wrestle with the music, herself and her dead husband. There were moments when the notes came with a dark undeniable magic, while at others the line would falter and die with her cursing at Charles and her inability to keep it together. But she would not give in, this musical utterance being born out of an unspeakable darkness, and within this cursed attitude, it took on something extraordinary. And as the storm continued to rage both inside and out, I became engrossed in the spectacle before me. Through what I can only describe as a mix of will and half-delirious inspiration, she pulled the score together for a considerably long stretch and it was impressive, truly unrepeatable, moments coming and going that made me wonder what music could actually become, or express.

It was a loud clap of thunder that broke the spell. She screamed with all her might at whoever might be listening, slammed down the keyboard lid, letting out an ungodly sound, and even in the flickering darkness I could see that she had hurt her hand, perhaps intentionally so.

But her torment wouldn't fade, for despite the pain she began to drift along beside the windows, back and forth through the whipping drapery, at one point pushing up the sash window even higher to invite the full force of the storm. And all the time she went on wailing and babbling, often incoherently, praising Charles and cursing herself, followed by cries of quite the contrary.

Eventually the possessed woman calmed down, but as I released myself from the spectacle and began to approach, she flung open the balcony doors and ran out into the blackness. For a brief moment I feared the worst: that she had thrown herself over the railings, but when I followed, she was there, teetering against the storm.

I pulled her back from the edge, but in an instant she lashed out and squirmed free, spun back through the doors, and after a few uncontrolled paces, fell to the parlour floor, howling and crying.

As her hysteria slipped into pathetic sobs, I busily locked the door and windows before running off to the bathroom to get a towel. Sitting down on the floor, I eased her onto my lap to clean her bloody hand and sweat-covered face, by then hardly able to recognise the woman I had come to know. We sat there for some time, listening to the rain in silence.

In her room, I bandaged her hand and dried her hair.

'You know, Sean... as I was playing, I began to feel... for the first time, that it was down there. The music, I mean,' she uttered in a broken whisper.

'One of those sure bets coming on,' was all I could say. As I put her into bed, she undid my trousers and pulled me in, and without another word we explored each other from head to toe.

AFTERNOON

The garden does something peculiar to the hours. What with this cast running from ankle to crotch, the weeds have been getting the better of me, although I have managed to rig up a gadget which gives some satisfaction. A modified litter grabber that I got from one of the town's street cleaners, the kind of thing which deftly picks up little popsicle sticks and chewing gum wrappers. For me it takes out weeds, or at least pulls their heads off, and with this in hand I edge my way slowly down the steps to my lawn disaster, which is finally on the mend.

'No grass yet,' I call in reference to our wager, turning from the newly seeded black earth to see Zeke washing his last bit of sandwich down with some iced tea – a drink which I have come to enjoy.

'Not sundown neither!' he calls back. 'And what about the Blue Bird ice cream?'

'Coming right up!' I reply, pleased to hear his request, knowing that he wouldn't have had the strength to call out like that, even a few days ago.

With some effort I fulfil my promise and the heavenly food silences us both.

'Have you any plans when you get out of that wheelchair?' I ask, scraping the creamy remains with a spoon before running my finger around the bowl with a temptation to lick it clean.

I watch Zeke roll the last bit of ice cream around his tongue. He doesn't answer, for no other reason that he is contemplating something else, gazing into his empty bowl before turning his attention towards me.

'Yeah, I know, I should have brought the rest of the carton,' I say. He doesn't press me.

'The Hanging Gardens of Babylon... do they still exist? Do they grow?' he asks, quite sincerely. At this he puts his head back, looks up into a cloud perched in front of the midday sun and closes his eyes. 'I have yet to cross the ocean... never been to the desert.'

I let him dream and in turn look back to the willow and the stream, different now with the sun overhead – everything mixed, bound up in a huge fine spray of light. Unconsciously I've picked up my pen.

...So, where did I leave off? Oh yes, asleep with Marion...

POSEIDON ON A
BLACK DOG DAY

I woke up from a dreamy sleep with, as it sometimes happens, the sweet smell of burning peat in my nostrils. Added to this was the rhythm of her breathing... my head on her thigh... only to fall back into the dream. And then sometime later, to Charles's words...

'Home... Home is where you start from.'

'Wha... what did you say?' she asked, half asleep.

'Oh... just something he once said.'

Our night's lovemaking had shunted me into a peculiarly heightened state – my whole body tingling, my mind as light and clear as I could ever remember.

'The storm?' she barely uttered.

'It's over now.' Yet thinking to myself: *or about to start.*

For if the pervious few months had been a gradual revelation of a man's past, the days that followed were to take on an unrestrained life of their own. As if I had been caught raw by the throat and forcibly ushered down some coiling shoot by one of those ancient Greek gods... Poseidon on a black dog day, revelling in the spectacle of a mere mortal blindly floundering in a boiling sea of time and action… Or to put it in a less fanciful way: the whole thing was ratcheting up.

I suppose the first warning, the first inkling, that things were about to get out of hand was what followed on from Charles's words. For his music had also returned and although it had come to me many times, there was something different, more insistent: no longer merely a guide but demanding an answer.

Could I have stayed in bed and left things at that? I guess not, for without further thought, I found myself sliding off the mattress and picking up my clothes.

By the time I was downstairs, a knot had taken hold in my stomach, for if I hadn't consciously admitted to what had to be done, some mute part of me must have known. On a detour through the parlour I picked up the bottle of bourbon, took a swig and put it into my pocket – still Charles's pocket, as far as I was concerned.

The storm had now passed and it was clear, the moon next to full, and to avoid waking Marion, I pushed the old Ford down the drive and popped the clutch. Luckily it started first time and I disappeared into the night.

I had the road to myself and under the silvery light I felt irrevocably unmoored. My mind passed over the string of incidents that had led me to this point and in what seemed no time that a clock could measure, I had found my way to the Aglaia's boundary. At an opportune spot I pulled off the highway, eased the creaky Ford under a large tree and turned off the complaining engine. This left nothing but the sound of my own mind mixed with a light breeze in the branches above, and I needed a little more help from the bottle of bourbon before stepping out into the warm fragrant air and scaling over the high stone wall.

The moonlight illuminated the wet undulating grass, the rolling hills seeming to glow greenish blue from within, and as I jogged along, I tried to keep under the trees as much as possible, checking for any sign of life before darting across the fairway. Near the maintenance shack, the machine that was going to make it all possible was sleeping in its place, and with the help of a small iron bar, I prized open the shack door and found the keyboard. Each was clearly marked in Zeke's handwriting, and I picked off *Old Digger*.

I had spent about a month on a similar machine when I was working for my uncle back in Chicago, and once seated in the cab with my hands on the controls, it all felt familiar. Apart from being out there at all I was concerned about two things: would there be enough juice in the battery to start, and would it have enough fuel to do the job?

I remember saying to myself out loud, 'You can still stop, put everything back, return to the car, and drive off. No one would be the wiser.' I don't know how long I stared at that key before I finally put it between forefinger and thumb and gave it a turn.

The battery had enough juice to turn over, but soon began to give out, the engine coughing and wheezing. I turned off the ignition and waited, someone somewhere having told me that it is better to try a weak battery in short spurts. The problem was, I still wasn't sure whether I wanted it to start at all. But I turned it again and on the third or fourth try, to my surprise the old diesel suddenly rattled to life, ripping into the silence of the night.

I was a few hundred yards along the service road before I

even took any notice of the fuel gauge. It wasn't that far from empty, so I made haste, so much so that I almost drove off the track and into some trees.

For a short time I got lost, but soon spotted a recognisable landmark that guided me in the direction of the fifteenth fairway. By then I was barrelling along in overdrive, and it wasn't long before the old magnolia appeared, silhouetted in the distance. And all the time I was worried about finding the exact line of the foundations, but if anything, the raking lights from the digger showed it up more clearly than the high light of day.

So here I was, about to do the unthinkable, asking myself if the powers that be offered the death penalty in the state of Georgia for mutilation of sacred ground.

'You could still stop!' I spoke aloud as the rusty toothed shovel hung ominously over the ground. And despite the roaring rattle of the machine, Charles's music came again, flooding into my head, and I eased the hydraulic handle and lowered the shovel into the soft manicured turf. Once it had gouged that first scar, there was no going back – digging deeper and wider, the music ever raging in my brain!

I must have dug down a good three or four feet before the shovel finally found the edge of the basement, but just when I began to scrape off what had to be the ground floor, a set of headlights flashed a reflection in the digger's glass. A moment of panic penetrated my brain but then came the thoughts of a man gone over, a man possessed: *what can they possibly do against such a machine? And anyway, I have nothing to lose now.*

From the corner of my eye, I saw Zeke and E emerging from the car almost before it had come to a stop, the old man waving his arms and screaming, not that I could possibly hear his words over the roar of the digger. Nor did it much matter, for I had no intention of stopping.

But it wasn't long before two police cars and an official Aglaia car also arrived. Out jumped Ned Barnes and even in the strange array of lights, I could tell his face was red with rage – something I took enjoyment from. Via the rear-view mirror I could see him shouting at Zeke, then suddenly the greenskeeper pushed him aside, got back into his car and started to drive it between me and the hole.

'Get the hell out of the way! I'm almost there!' I shouted as we jostled for position.

But he wouldn't give in. Everywhere I went he spun his shiny new car into my way. Frustration exploded into anger, and I brought the shovel down under the car's rear end to try to slide him sideways. But just at the wrong time, the lever slipped through my fingers and the digger lunged forwards, and before I knew it, Zeke and his car were sliding into the hole. I tried desperately to hold back the car, but this only made matters worse, mutilating its side and smashing a window.

Suddenly Zeke's safety became all important, and as I backed off a policeman ran in front with a shot gun and a moment later another jumped up on the side of the cab. I remember looking around into the black barrel of a revolver – the first time I had ever seen a handgun out of its holster.

'Cut the engine! Now!' the man shouted.

Hearing his order, there was a moment when I very nearly revved the throttle, and I'm still not sure what stopped me, although I swear there were men screaming and they were not those around me. For what I heard was Gaelic, and to this day I believe it was the sound of my father and his shipmates desperately calling out to each other in the midst of a devouring sea.

At that point I must have gone into a kind of daze, for the next thing I remember was being hauled down from the digger by my hair and dragged across the ground. And when they lifted me to my feet, Ned Barnes came charging forward, his hands stretched out towards my neck. One of the officers had to hold him at bay, as the other shoved me into the back of a police car.

'What is down there is mine!' I screamed at the president of the Aglaia National.

'Get him out of here! Or you will be taking both of us to jail!' he screamed with murder in his eyes, froth spilling from the corner of his mouth.

And as the police car pulled away, I glanced back to see E climbing down into the hole to rescue Zeke. I had certainly left them one hell of a mess.

VAGUE GUESSES TO
FORGOTTEN QUESTIONS

The ride to the police station was swift and silent. No sirens, for as I was to learn, they didn't want such an outrageous story getting around. The two lawmen unceremoniously threw me into a small cell and turned out the lights. Unbelievable as it may sound, only then did I begin to grasp what sort of mess I had landed myself in.

As I lay in that damp shapeless void in what felt a long, dark, distorted tunnel out of time, my mind became an unfettered flow of unruly notions, ploughing through me like I was some sort of badly planned junction. Inventions in my mind's ear came, went and came again. Charles's music – this time an oppressive invasion, for by then I was ready to accuse his expressions of causing me nothing but torment – a musical mirage which had led me a dance into hell. And the fishermen returned but overlaying their last calls in the sea swell was a kind of keening – if I'm not mistaken, a free verse lament for the dead.

In those deadly hours I drifted in and out of sleep – hardly sleep, for conscious or not my mind would not rest, would not stay still. Dream became entwined into thought, as it in turn would slip back into dream, the manner of which made it impossible to know one from the other. So much came and went, yet how little I am now able to recall. This said, for some inexplicable reason one image has stuck, of eight, maybe ten grey men sitting on a bench. Their heads, most of them, cocked to the left. On occasion one would turn to another, and as he did, his face, even his whole head, would alter, transform into someone else... as if all perception was relative, dependent upon a point of view, or that through the meeting, through the encounter, one or both were changed.

Again, I heard the men screaming and yet towards the end of those twisted hours of mental contrivance, a brief but persuasive lucidity rose up, hinting at some inexplicable riddle. And yet in groping for more, it drifted away, slipped through my mind's fumbling fingers to leave nothing but a smoky darkness.

By the time the grey dawn emerged through the rusty bars of the solitary window, I couldn't even recall what this construction had been about, let alone any sort of potential enlightenment. My brain, nothing but a spongy matrix of suspect inventions... vague guesses at forgotten questions... dim echoes of past encounters, encounters in which the very recollection seemed to cloud any meaning, any sort of deeper understanding that I seemed to crave. And when, with all my will, I tried to blow it clean, the only notion that came to my lips was the word "contrary". Like some boiled-down cipher or leftover carcass which had been picked bare. Strength and weakness... the stillness and the dance... the end and the beginning. All interchangeable in the blink of a watery eye.

And into this came the gun, as once more my mind's eye ran down the barrel of the man's black revolver to meet his stare, eyes intent upon ending my life if I gave him the slightest excuse, if I so chose.

And truth knows, I was a mere breath from inviting their purpose... no doubt a relative of that unreasonable monster who wanted to turn its destruction on the garden. As if there was another reality which I give cause to surface when the time is wrong... or right. The desire, the need, to push the material too far... to make it stretch, to let it snap...

And so, does this division break or make the whole? Reflect upon a blackness... merge with the illumination. A link, possibly. A *hint*... That to be *one* I must be broken, taken apart... tossed into a sea... the slated sounds of the sirens my only counsel.

Be this as it may, towards the end of this peculiar mental stacking came the smell of rain, then its soothing sound – light at first, but by the time the daylight had coaxed out some sort of form in the almost colourless room, it had turned to a relieving downpour. The rough cement wall was the only other distraction, but as my gaze wandered over its patterns, accusatory demons emerged, pointing their distorted fingers at my folly. That through such an obsession I had concocted an absurd task and ended up a ridiculous criminal. And what I had done to Zeke was inexcusable.

The only thing that came close to consoling me was the thought of Marion. There was something impressive about her when I had left her asleep. I had grown to respect her, to love her. And to my surprise she had shown great tenderness. Such courage too, growing out of the poisoned creature which had left me standing on her doorstep only a few months before. Oh, that meanness could still surface, but it was no longer quite the same. And besides, I couldn't help thinking that this strange pride of hers had something to do with the change… although I cannot begin to argue such a notion. What I did know was that despite herself, she had chosen to *act* upon what she knew had to be done, and had *given*, to herself, to the garden, to Charles and to me. And through it all she was liberated and had changed. At that moment it seemed a rare thing, especially as I was so imprisoned, not only by that cell but by my own self-inflicted incarceration.

When I did finally manage to give in, to shut down and sleep, the chief of police and one of my near executioners entered my cell.

'Ned Barnes has cooled down some and he wants this boy out of the county. Put him on the next bus for Atlanta. And Bert, I sure as hell don't want this getting around.'

I was so glad to be lifted up out of there, taken to a washroom where Officer Bert helped to clean me up. He showed no malice, and if truth be known I think part of him was amused, refreshed by the novelty of it all – perhaps the first time he had ever had the privilege to set foot on Aglaia's sacred ground. But his mean-looking partner was another matter, betraying a certain enjoyment in crunching a pair of handcuffs too far into my wrists and pushing me hard into the back of a patrol car.

In silence we drove the few blocks to the Aglaia bus depot. And I remember thinking how they were certainly doing a quick job of getting rid of the evidence.

'Don't you ever come back here,' that cruel mouth advised as he firmly ushered me to the back seat of the bus.

They both waited and watched, beady-eyed in the patrol car, while a few more passengers got on. I thought the bus would never start up and just when its engine coughed into life, an off-duty driver hopped on, he and the driver chatting away like long-lost friends. The creaky old machine grunted through the pot-holed street, some pots so deep that it felt like its axle would break with the strain. The police car followed a short distance behind, pulling over at the edge of town before doing a slow U-turn.

I remember overhearing a black couple who were sitting a few seats away, talking amongst themselves.

'Yeah... I'm telling you, his car was stolen, and he has bought another,' she said, elbowing her depressed-looking husband.

'And where the hell did Joey get the money to buy a brand new one?' he barely asked.

'The car! Marion's car. You idiot,' I suddenly remembered under my breath, the realisation pricking my tired, ragged mind into life. *Just leave it where it is and come back for it later*, was what it then proposed, remembering too well the lawman's warning. *But it might not even be there when you return*, came the following argument, and at that moment I never wanted to see this place again. As my mind tossed the debate to and fro, the off-duty driver pointed towards a crossroad and prepared to be let off. It was a now or never, and although I was still not sure, I silently moved up to the seat next to the back door. My hope was that when he was let off, this door would also swing open and with any luck I would slip away, and no one would be the wiser. I waited what seemed an age for the bus to shift down and grind to a stop, but as the men said their farewells, the door didn't budge. In a panic I went for the only button in sight and to my surprise it slid apart with a loud thwack. And as everyone turned in my direction, I sprung off that seat like a jackrabbit, jumping blindly down onto soft gravel, into a watery ditch, up the other side and on through some thorny bushes.

Scratched and dizzy, it took me a little time to get my bearings, all the while worrying about whether the bus driver would bother to inform the police about my hasty departure. By the time I had got to the Aglaia Golf Club's boundary road, I was wet through and feeling rough as hell, with every pair of headlights feeling like a prowling police car.

To my relief the Ford was still there, under the shadows of the trees. Inside I immediately went for the bourbon in the glove box, guzzling away most of the bottle. It calmed me, so much so that the gravity of what I had done to Zeke loomed back into my conscience. Did he survive unhurt from his smashed-up car? I could hardly tolerate my mind's inventions, and this together with the growing effects of the bourbon must have put me out.

A clap of thunder eventually brought me around, the drink having left me with a throbbing head, and yet it didn't stop me from finishing the bottle. My single intention was to get back to the mansion in one piece… how little I knew of what was in store.

Things did not begin well, for after persuading myself that I could drive in a straight line, I reversed into a large tree and almost got stuck in the mud before the old car spun around and heaved back onto the highway. Passing the Aglaia gate, I again felt this horrendous pang of guilt for what I had done to Zeke, and it was then, to my dreaded disbelief, that I saw a police car come cruising out of its entrance. The sight was far too much for my loose mind and in a panic, I slouched down and moved away. My departure must have been a little too fast, for when I looked in the rear-view mirror, the car was closing from behind. As we passed a number of side roads, I hoped against hope that the lawman would turn off, but no such luck, for not only did he stay with me, he narrowed the gap between us and began to flash his lights.

I guess a little more speed turned into a getaway, for the next thing I knew we were both barrelling along a dipping, twisting road through the blinding sheets of rain. With his lights still flashing, I desperately tried to keep from slipping into the ditch, and as we roared over a hill, a large deer, antlers and all, froze in my headlights! Breaking hard, I went into a wild skid, yet as I braced myself for the collision, the animal disappeared, bounding out of my path with nothing to spare. And the surprising thing was, in all my panic and confusion, it was my pursuer who had caught the gravel shoulder, and as I regained control and sped onto an old iron bridge, he skidded off the road, missing the buttress by inches before sliding down the bank and into a rising river.

YU... YURISH

At the sight of the car disappearing at the bridge, I slammed on the brakes and backed up, looking out in horror as the driver struggled to open his door into the torrent. It was only then that I realised it was not the police at all, but Zeke in an official Aglaia car!

Just as the wreck began to roll and slip away into the rapids, he squeezed out, and to the sound of his incoherent cries, I scrambled down to the river's edge, grabbed a long branch and waded in towards him. By this time he had got some sort of a grip on a jutting rock but in lunging for the lifeline, he came off with such a force that it pulled me into the swirling current. To my horror, we were now both drifting down-river.

I remember screaming at him, the current pulling even harder when we slammed into a big rock and our branch snapped in two. That same rock abruptly stopped my descent, but Zeke got swept around and after trying to clear my lungs, I followed, certain that he would never make it on his own.

Luckily I soon caught up, pulled him close and got his face clear of the water. Not long after that the river eased its descent into a turn, and we were pushed into some snags. I worked our way towards the river's edge, and only then did I realise that my leg was in a bad way. Still, I somehow managed to drag us free of the muddy deluge, up onto the slimy bank, and after trying to get the water out of the old man's lungs, I must have passed out.

When I came to, my legs were actually bobbing in the rising current, with Zeke unconscious but still breathing. Towering above was a high rock face, so the best I could do was to pull us up another foot or so, and as I lay there, staring up at the thick sky, trying to put our diminishing chances out of my mind, Zeke's cries near the bridge returned to my thoughts. What had he been trying to say before he passed out? *Yur... Yurish*, something like that; this in turn calling up the Banshee's words from the recesses of my memory, the calls of young Dearbhla Flood before I fled her house. *And what of your wish?* The last thing she spoke as the church bells finished the hour and I made off in desperate pursuit of my father's boat. Yes... *And what of your wish?* And to the sound of the water and, if I am not mistaken, a whine in the rigging, my memory opened up...

* * *

With the church bells echoing, young Sean runs! Runs as fast as his legs will carry him! Along the shoreline, over the rocks... sand and more sand. It seems further than ever before. All to no avail, for as he rounds the cove, the boat is heading out to sea, no doubt the captain wondering where his son has got to. At that, Sean's legs give way, disappointment opening the gates to exhaustion and as his lungs scream for air, he trips and falls in the sand. He lies there for some time, for when he staggers to his feet the sky has become darker, much darker, the sun dipping into the sea.

Despondent, he passes the outcrops of coastal rocks that pierce the golden strand and feeling ever more aimless, he wanders for some while. The tide is approaching but he fails to take notice, doesn't much care, taunting the rising waters, so much so that when he eventually raises his downturned head towards the shore, the sea has laid its trap.

It is a big spring tide, the west wind its ally. Perhaps he could swim it, but by now the sun is all but down, the tide-race black, cold, and pulling hard. As the dry sand dissolves, he climbs onto a rock, and with that wind ever rising, he watches the clouds, low and dark, rolling in, as if released from the offing. And it's getting colder, yet his mother will have little reason to concern herself, believing her son to be safe on-board her husband's boat.

The cliffs are alive to the collisions of the huge rollers, the lashings of white froth spilling down. Fingers growing numb, he removes the fossil from his pocket that he found earlier in the day. When the moon shows itself through a break in the clouds, he can see a fair distance – almost to his grandad's. Perhaps he is playing his fiddle, cosy by the fire. What young Sean would give to be by the fire... He thinks again about diving in, making for the disappearing shore. He hesitates, the voluted rock slipping from his stiffening wet fingers, falling tic-tac into a gaping black fissure. In reaching down into the darkness, he loses his footing, and for the first time a strange smell wells up into his nostrils...

* * *

So there it is, or was. I had passed out in a fit of epilepsy, had never made it to the boat, having lain on that rock all night, desperately clutching my ammonite fossil in the raging storm.

The story goes that the next morning an old woman almost stepped on me while out digging for clams. Seemingly, I had survived when all others had perished. Rumours spread as rumours do: 'He is blessed! Delivered from death itself!'... 'The boy is cursed! His first fishing run and six able fishermen are lost!' The fact that I couldn't remember a thing, one way or another, was all the better for those who invented their own accounts. As for me, I may not have been lost at sea but felt drowned by the misery, the horror of it all.

And with the water still rising, I pulled Zeke up a few more inches, by now tight against the rock face with nowhere else to go.

YOUR GODDAMNED WISH!

The last thing I recall at the river's edge was watching the milky waters carry my trickling blood away, and by that time I wasn't sure if Zeke was still alive. I'm told two hunters happened by before the rising river swept us from our precarious mooring, although I have not as yet met with our saviours. In my mind's eye they are Poseidon's workmen, perhaps Proteus and one of his mates, and for this I will never say another word against the great god.

It was two or three days before I came to, as it happened in the very same hospital ward that had tended my last attack of epilepsy. The biggest relief of my life was to look across and see Zeke in the next bed – unconscious but still alive. And as soon as I was able to stand, Marion took me back to the mansion and not long afterwards we began to make our daily trip to the hospital, me to stay and watch over Zeke while she went on to her job in Atlanta. As I stood guard over the motionless old man, great relief gradually turned to hope, which as the days passed became shaded with doubt.

On one overcast morning, after almost a week of this, she was not feeling too well, having had a dizzy spell the night before. What made matters worse was that I was letting my sense of morbidity get the better of me, feeling more depressed as each passing day presented no sign that Zeke would ever come out of his coma. And the medics in all their honesty could not offer much hope in the matter of his chances. Still, we both put on a brave face and went along to the hospital, yet as soon as we set foot in the place Marion almost fell over from another dizzy spell. Since the river accident she had not stopped – her life divided between her job, looking after me and spending what little energy she had left working in the garden. Time and time again I told her to leave the weeds, but she wouldn't tolerate their return. On top of this she had lost her appetite and as I was telling her off for not eating enough, one of the nurses took charge and rolled her away in a wheelchair.

As before, there was no change in Zeke's condition and taking my usual chair next to his bedside, I soon dozed off. It was sometime later that I was woken – not by a staff nurse eager to clear the wards, but by the very hand of Zeke, his outstretched arm gently brushing the top of my head! We know in our mind that life is a miracle, yet it rarely feels that way, but that moving hand and those open eyes certainly did and I couldn't stop the tears rolling down from mine.

I propped him up with another pillow and it wasn't long before he was attempting to say something, yet try as he might, nothing much would come out.

'Just take it easy,' I pleaded, holding a glass of water to his dried lips. He took a long drink before laying back, slowly opening and closing his eyes as if he couldn't quite believe that he had returned to the land of the living. I sat there a bit dumbstruck, unable to credit that he was there, awake in front of my eyes, and just as I was about to ring for a nurse, he beckoned me close.

'The c... ca... car,' he barely whispered.

'The car? It is still in the river. But that is the least of your worries,' I assured him.

'In the trun...' he tried, his eyes widening with anxious excitement.

'What's that?' I questioned, putting the glass to his lips and making sure he took another drink.

'Yuish,' he eventually tried again before clearing his throat. And again, I gave him more water and waited for his pronouncement, for I now knew that he simply had to make himself understood. And eventually the passionate whisper came. 'Your... your goddamned wish! I found it!'

'Your wish! My wish! You found the music? And it is still in the car? In the trunk of the car... somewhere down-river!'

As his pronouncement began to sink in, Marion entered the ward with a little more colour in her cheeks, and at the sight of Zeke she couldn't hold her emotions at bay, kneeling down and placing her head in the old man's lap. What followed as he kept eyeing his surroundings was a silence of gratefulness, this only broken when a nurse came to the aid of the reborn man and somewhat officiously showed us the exit. I promised him we would return in the morning.

During the drive back to the mansion, my mind became a confused whirl of contradictions. While watching over Zeke there had been plenty of time to contemplate my reckless actions – that in the cold light of reason, if anyone had suggested doing what I had done, I would surely have declared their madness. And even though my hunch about the rest of the music had come up trumps, the need to fight for it had dimmed. The unnerving night in jail, together with the river that had taken us within a thin breath of Hades, had put paid to my courage. I'll admit that as soon as Zeke made his pronouncement, a familiar voice spoke up in favour of pursuing the music, yet this was accompanied by a chorus of those elders from Baile na Bhaid: '...the waters will take him... will have him yet.' And despite telling myself that their talk was soaked in superstition, when all was weighed up, I believe I'd have let the bounty rest in its watery grave. It was while wrestling with this private conundrum that Marion suddenly broke the silence.

'Charles,' she said, in a way that sent a shudder through me – that for some reason, *he* had suddenly taken my place. She drove on quite sensibly. I said nothing, waiting for her to continue the conversation. 'The first and the last thing I heard you say. You remember. The concert in the church, before you ever heard me play... and at the end, while you waited for a taxi and I was in the kitchen baking bread. God knows why. Something to push into... I heard your hat hit the floor beside the piano stool, the way you used to take it off as you sat down. What was it? Schubert... the, the andantino... D958 or 959? No more than a few minutes. How did you expect me to carry on after that? Me with my wet dough.'

I did not feel like interrupting, nor did I need to, for the on-rush of a passing truck soon brought her back and she turned to me, by now very much in the moment.

'Plastic bag,' she said. 'That's what Zeke whispered into my ear before that nurse swept us off the ward. "In a plastic bag."'

With a certain trepidation I explained the revelation, believing that he'd hauled the manuscript out of the buried basement. I watched her eyes begin to intensify.

'So the music is there, in that car! And we are to assume that Zeke has tied it up in a plastic bag! And that we… you have been right all along!' she exclaimed with a mixture of pride and more than a hint of ill feeling for Ned Barnes and his rubber-stamping committee members. 'Self-important wind bags! Every one of them!'

I can still hear myself agreeing with her about me being right, but as it turned out, this wasn't even true. As Zeke was to admit with more than a hint of embarrassment a few days later.

'I'll be dammed if I didn't have it all along!' He admitted, going on to explain that at the very time I was sneaking across the fairways on my mission of exhumation, he was woken up by Charles's music. 'Marion's playing that day at the club had got to me, more than I knew,' is the way he put it. And he hadn't been awake for more than a few seconds when he had the strongest feeling that the first movement was somewhere near, saying that around the time that Hector was being evicted from the nursery, he had presented Zeke with his horticultural notes, old seed catalogues and the like. On my one visit to Zeke's house I had noticed them, several volumes taking pride of place on his mantlepiece. And over the years Zeke had put them to good use, but to his shame he had left the rest of the material in the back of his garage, all stacked up in two old tea chests, untouched since the day they arrived.

So, while I was on my way to dig that hole, he was down on his hands and knees going through heaps of old catalogues and trade magazines, and near the bottom of one of those chests, along with a few of Charles's schoolbooks and scholastic ribbons, he eventually found it! The music! A little mouldy but safe and sound. 'God knows if Hector even remembered it was there!' was what Zeke reckoned.

But driving back from the hospital with both of us feeling vindicated, I wasn't taking much notice of our surroundings – that is until Marion slowed the car and turned onto a little-used road.

'What are you doing? Where are you going?' I had to ask.

'Where do you think!' she answered in a clear steady voice.

'Are you crazy?!' I suddenly realised. 'The car, or what's left of it, is probably no bigger than an armchair by now. And six feet underwater!'

'You said you had noticed it some ways down from where you and Zeke got out.'

'I wouldn't depend upon the evidence of such a witness. Hallucinations were the order of the moment by then. And anyway, it probably didn't rest there. And even if it isn't underwater, we are going to need some help!'

'Help!' she called out at the passing bullrushes. 'The only person who has ever been of any help is lying in a hospital bed!'

'Look at me!' I remember screaming back. 'I'm on crutches for Chrissake! I'm useless!'

But by then she would not listen, and as if nature was just waiting for its queue, the heavens opened up and the rain began to thunder down.

'It's starting again. It may be our last chance.'

'It may be our last act!' I screamed. Yet despite my objections, she drove on, foot to the floor.

The woman who had nearly passed out from lack of strength not but an hour or so before was now charging through the pelting rain like a stoked locomotive.

THE RETURN

Once I knew that Marion was not going to be swayed, I went back to bragging about how I had been right all along and how little those rich, stuffed shirts knew about anything. I meant every word of it, but in truth it was but a smokescreen to keep me from thinking about where we were going, not to mention what we could possibly do if we actually found the wreck. But we drove on into the sodden countryside and after I had misdirected Marion several times, we eventually arrived at the bridge. From there we set off on foot, taking a little used track that ran towards the spot where I had dragged Zeke out.

'So what did the doctor say?' I asked, glimpsing the churning water through the passing trees – for me, the River Styx itself.

'Oh, they just laid me down on a bed and gave me something to drink. So are we close?' she asked, more interested in the subject at hand.

It wasn't long before we found a place to stop and we were sliding down a high bank, me with crutches in hand, trying to keep from falling head over heels. Slippery was an understatement, and I couldn't keep my eyes off the watery snake of swelling water. We eventually passed the spot where we had been rescued and as the current grew heavier, I peered in vain for any sight of the wreck. By that time, those deadly familiar waters had got to me good and proper, and my morbid mind wouldn't stop turning back to the shores of Donegal and the elders' fateful words.

'It must have been swept further down,' I reasoned, all the while thinking it was likely to be underwater by now. So, with difficulty, we made our way further along the bank, more often than not my crutches sinking into the sodden earth, tiring my arms something fierce. Then just when it was all looking futile, Marion, who had worked her way ahead, called out, having spotted the car's back end sticking out amongst a group of rocks. As we approached the battered piece of rusting metal, she looked at me, knowing full well that I didn't stand a chance of attempting it, that I wasn't going to be much use.

'We can go back for some help,' I suggested, angry at my broken leg and the fact that we had gotten drawn into such a dreadful scene.

'This rain is here to stay.'

She was right. The water was rising fast, and it was likely to be the only chance we would get. We studied the numerous rocks of various sizes that separated us, while between them the opaque waters coiled and rumbled in an ever increasing torrent. I will never forget what she said next.

'Take off your shoes,' she ordered. 'Come on, mine have heels and yours are rubber soled.'

'Charles's shoes,' I reminded her as she helped me untie them, the one just there for show below my cast. Although they were far too big for her, with both pairs of socks and tightly tied, they were just about okay.

'I don't want you to go. If you slip off into that water, I can't see me being much help. We can still turn back,' I pleaded.

As Marion stood there, by now soaked to the bone, I felt such affection for her and if truth be known, I was very willing to let the music go. And then, while I was adjusting my footing in the sticky mud, she suddenly turned away and took a leap to the first stone... and then the second.

'I want it as much as you... maybe more!' she called out before jumping to the next.

Every detail of her trial is indelibly etched in my mind, probably because of my inability to be of any use, to be condemned to watch while all the time thinking that like the excavation, I should never have taken it this far. And then, as if by my fear alone, it very nearly happened. She slipped as she landed from a long leap and her foot slid and jammed underwater. In a panic she pulled hard, which only wedged the big shoe tighter. Taking a deep breath she pulled again, gradually squeezing her foot free to leave socks and all. Marion quickly shed the other shoe and continued in her bare feet, and I breathed again when she made the final jump and grabbed hold of the wreck.

She took a few moments to gather herself and when she tried the trunk lid it wouldn't budge, being either locked or jammed from all the contortion.

'The keys!' I shouted. 'They must be in the ignition!'

She tried the only door that was clear and when that wouldn't open, she grabbed a rock and smashed the window.

'Get all the glass out!' was all I could offer before she wiggled through the window, her head and torso going down into the cold water. And a few seconds later she came struggling out, coughed and sputtered before gathering herself together and going back through again.

On her return, I thought she had again come up empty-handed, but as she crouched down to catch her breath, she held up the keys. That's when the car creaked and shifted, and for a moment I thought for sure it was going to float back into the current. At first Marion didn't seem to notice, but suddenly she jumped up and, in an instant, had the key in the lock. But again, it wouldn't budge and in desperation she wheeled around, grabbed another rock and with great effort whacked upwards against the number plate. To my amazement, the lid sprung free!

'Nothing!' came Marion's first muffled cry as she rummaged around in the dark hole.

But then, as she turned into what little light there was, she held up a large black plastic bag and made a funny little squeak of triumph. When she undid the knot and pulled out some papers, I witnessed her smile, even from such a distance through the pouring rain.

And yet as she headed back, I don't know whether it was just her excitement or what, but before I knew it, she had disappeared, had slipped off and gone under. To my relief she bobbed up to become pinned to a stone and without even a thought of what to do, I was moving into the river.

'Let it go! Let the music go! Or try and pitch it onto one of the rocks!' I urged, knowing full well that while holding onto it she stood little chance of clambering back onto the stone. But the woman would have none of it. 'Come on! We can get it later!' I urged again.

Still, she refused, knowing full well that there would

be little hope of recovering it if it got into the water. So, I judged the river's depth and hobbled in deeper, yet by the time I was up to my waist, there was still a fair distance between us. In trying to close the gap the current began to pull me over. I didn't resist, but instead pushed hard with the crutch and used the water's force to take me to her. I didn't make it but did get a foothold on the next rock but one. In the meantime, she was still floundering like some desperate animal, and I remember suddenly feeling so damned angry, stretching out my crutch and screaming for her to throw me the bag.

'No! We'll lose it for sure!' she screamed back, again trying to get clear of the water.

'Throw it upstream then! And let it come to me!' was all I could think of.

When at last she flung it, I stretched as far as I dared and just managed to snag enough of the bag to keep it from floating away.

'Just keep against the rock and don't move!' I remember ordering, wedging myself half out of the water, all the time fearing that at any moment she would lose the fight and disappear. That's when I got the idea of blowing up the bag with air, tying it off and re-tying it to the end of my crutch, so it became a sort of float which would help to keep the crutch and my tired arm from sinking. This done, I pushed myself to the next rock and stretched the desperate idea out to her.

But she still needed that one leap of faith, would have to let go of her rock to commit to the end of the crutch.

Of course, Zeke and I had been here before, and I feared that the force of her lunge might send us both into the insistent current. With a look of terror, she tried once more to clamber onto the stone but again with the same pathetic result. I looked into her dark exhausted eyes, and to be honest, I wouldn't have bet on her chances.

EVENING

The afternoon has gone and with the first cool breeze, I make my way down the steps towards the newly seeded lawn. The sun, now solid red, has lowered itself behind the black willow, the stream only heard. True to Zeke's wishes, the water sprinkler has been doing its job, yet the earth looks as black as the day it was seeded.

'Five dollars, if you please!' I call out to my friend, he being back on the balcony with his nose firmly buried in the newspaper, no doubt in a final attempt on that nagging crossword.

'Have a closer look!' he answers.

I do as he says, and I swear that the little pricks of grass have just come up on his command! I crouch down even lower to make sure that he hasn't persuaded me of things that do not exist... but damned if he isn't right. A few thin sprinkles of faint green are dotted here and there over the dark surface – the tips of tiny needles catching what remains of the evening light. I say nothing and return to the balcony, he no doubt sensing the meaning of my silence.

'A ghostly double,' he murmurs in frustration, 'twelve letters.'

'I've never been much good at crosswords,' I admit, uncrumpling a five dollar bill from my pocket and putting it into his outstretched hand.

My gaze returns to the notebook, and to my shame I've managed little of any consequence. *In those strange moments I had no idea where I was, nor for that matter who I was,* catching my eye. Most of the rest, as the saying goes, has been written on water.

Still, it doesn't lessen the fact that these past few months have been an odyssey for me. Certainly I've learnt plenty about the man who instigated it, who spoke out from his dream while I lay in darkness, seemingly with no way forward nor back. And he has given me a great deal, not least a portion of my past that I doubtless would never have come to know.

Yet there is more to it, and I return to our short time together. For the lack of anything more definite, there was a *rightness* about it. An awareness in the encounter, intent and action, which demanded nothing… yet required everything. And in the giving we were found… changed. Destroyed and created. I him and he me… well, something like that.

Zeke turns his head to the faint sound of the front door as it opens and closes. We wait in anticipation and a figure eventually emerges from the darkness of the parlour.

'You are back early,' he calls out in surprise.

'Yes,' is all Marion admits, pausing to look down at the only remaining question in his crossword. 'Doppelganger,' she says with little hesitation before turning in my direction. 'And what is that you have there?'

'A notebook. I have been trying to recall these past six months.'

'Doppelganger?' Zeke concedes, completing the puzzle.

'I very much doubt if anyone would believe such a tale, Sean. And besides...' she continues, removing her jacket and walking back into the parlour.

'Ever since I have known that woman, she has had a habit of doing that,' Zeke complains.

'What, butting in on your crosswords?'

'No, stopping in mid-sentence! Right when she has raised my interest!'

In irritation he turns his wheelchair and pushes himself towards the balcony door. There is a small step that although he always tries his damnedest to roll up and over, he can never quite manage. So I give him a hand, and we follow her into the parlour.

'Besides what, Marion?' Zeke insists.

Pretending not to hear, she pulls her thick brown hair back with both hands before sitting down at the piano – a habit she has before playing. We wait in silence while she arranges the soiled sheets of music on the stand. The dark middle movement comes to the top, the one that used to present such difficulty. Marion begins. Zeke's look of frustration struggles in vain against the power of the notes. And after a page or so of the most beautiful playing, she stops and looks up in the strangest way. I wouldn't begin to know how to describe it, other than to say that I don't believe a man could ever come up with such an expression.

'And besides what?' Zeke asks again.

'And besides,' she repeats, looking back to the music, 'the story isn't finished.'

'What do you mean?' we both want to know.

Again, she ignores our pleas, turning back to the beginning

of the sonata. I bend over her, thinking that the answer to this apparent riddle might be found in the music. We all look at the first bold marks of the nineteen-year-old Charles, and despite the mouldy water stains, the passionate, driving toccata stands out proudly from the page.

'Because…' She hesitates. 'I have been to the doctor.'

Yes? we scream with our eyes.

'As usual, he checked my bruises.'

'Yes. Go on.'

'He also informed me… that I am going to have a child.'

We are having one of our silences. Even Zeke is lost for words.

Marion is wiping her eyes with little success. My brain has stopped. Cheeks wet, she lowers her outstretched hands onto the keyboard, takes a breath and begins to play, attacking the music with the gusto of the young man who had composed it some forty-odd years past.

And she doesn't stop there, giving us the whole work… something that no one has ever done, nor heard, before.

The author was born on the Canadian Prairies in Brandon Manitoba in 1953. He has lived in the UK since the age of twenty, where he trained as a violin maker/restorer and subsequently became a founding partner of Oxford Violins. Amongst his interests are writing, painting and film.

This book is printed on paper from sustainable sources managed under the Forest Stewardship Council (FSC) scheme.

It has been printed in the UK to reduce transportation miles and their impact upon the environment.

For every new title that Troubador publishes, we plant a tree to offset CO_2, partnering with the More Trees scheme.

For more about how Troubador offsets its environmental impact, see www.troubador.co.uk/sustainability-and-community